Chloe jumped. She whirled toward the sound but could see nothing. "Thank you, but I'm fine."

"You sure?" A figure emerged from the nearby trees, a deep shadow moving closer.

"I can manage." As she spoke, her fist reached for the small canister of pepper spray she carried. If this guy got much closer, he was going to get a face full of pain.

"I'm sure you can, but Opal ordered me over here to help. So here I am ready to lend a hand."

"Opal shouldn't have bothered you, Mr....?"

"Ben Avery. And it wasn't a bother."

She'd heard plenty about the handsome widower who pastored Grace Christian Church. It had led Chloe to believe he was in his late fifties or early sixties. He looked closer to thirty, his hair just a little too long, his leather jacket more biker than preacher.

"I'm sure you have other things to do, Pastor Avery."

"I can't think of any offhand. And call me Ben."

Books by Shirlee McCoy

Love Inspired Suspense

Die Before Nightfall #5
Even in the Darkness #14
When Silence Falls #18
Little Girl Lost #40
Valley of Shadows #61
Stranger in the Shadows #76

Steeple Hill Trade

Still Waters

SHIRLEE McCOY

has always loved making up stories. As a child she daydreamed elaborate tales in which she was the heroine—gutsy, strong and invincible. Though she soon grew out of her superhero fantasies, her love for storytelling never diminished. She knew early that she wanted to write inspirational fiction, and began writing her first novel when she was a teenager. Still, it wasn't until her third son was born that she truly began pursuing her dream of being published. Three years later she sold her first book. Now a busy mother of four, Shirlee is a homeschool mom by day and an inspirational author by night. She and her husband and children live in Maryland and share their house with a dog and a guinea pig. You can visit her Web site at www.shirleemccoy.com.

STRANGER IN THE SHADOWS

Shirlee McCoy

Steeple
Hill®

Published by Steeple Hill Books™

STEEPLE HILL BOOKS

Steeple
Hill®

ISBN-13: 978-0-373-44266-9
ISBN-10:   0-373-44266-1

STRANGER IN THE SHADOWS

Copyright © 2007 by Shirlee McCoy

www.SteepleHill.com

Printed in U.S.A.

Send forth your light and your truth,
let them guide me; let them bring me to your
holy mountain, to the place where you dwell.
—*Psalms* 43:3

To Brenda Minton who makes me laugh when I
want to cry. Thanks for the brainstorming sessions
and the pep talks, but mostly thanks for being you.

And to Bob and Jan Porter and
Dick and Carolyn Livesey who are
true encouragers.
Thanks for always cheering me on!

ONE

It came in the night, whispering into her dreams. Silent stars, hazy moonlight, a winding road. Sudden, blinding light.

Impact.

Rolling, tumbling, terror. And then silence.

Smoke danced at the edges of memory as flames writhed serpentlike through cracked glass and crumbled metal, hissing and whirling in the timeless dance of death.

Adam! She reached for his hand, wanting to pull him from the car and from the dream—whole and alive. Safe. But her questing hand met empty space and hot flame, her body flinching with the pain and the horror of it.

Sirens blared in the distance, their throbbing pulse a heartbeat ebbing and flowing with the growing flames. She turned toward the door, trying to push aside hot, bent metal, and saw a shadow beyond the shattered glass; a dark figure leaning toward the window, staring in. Dark eyes that seemed to glow in the growing flames.

Help me! She tried to scream the words, but they caught in her throat. And the shadow remained still and silent, watching as the car burned and she burned with it.

* * *

The shrill ring of an alarm clock sounded over the roar of flames, spearing into Chloe Davidson's consciousness and pulling her from the nightmare. For a moment there was nothing but the dream. No past. No present. No truth except hot flames and searing pain. But the flames weren't real, the pain a fading memory. Reality was…what?

Chloe scrambled to anchor herself in the present before she fell back into the foggy world of unknowns she'd lived in during the weeks following the accident.

"Saturday. Lakeview, Virginia. The Morran wedding. Flowers. Decorations." She listed each item as it came to mind, grabbing towels from the tiny closet beside the bathroom door, pulling clothes from her dresser. Black pants. Pink shirt. Blooming Baskets' uniform. Her new job. Her new life. A normality she still didn't quite believe in.

The phone rang before she could get in the shower, the muted sound drawing her from the well-lit bedroom and into the dark living room beyond.

"Hello?" She pressed the receiver to her ear as she flicked on lamps and the overhead light, her heart still racing, her throbbing leg an insistent reminder of the nightmare she'd survived.

"Chloe. Opal, here."

At the sound of her friend and boss's voice, Chloe relaxed, leaning her hip against the sofa and forcing the dream and the memories to the back of her mind. "You've only been gone a day and you're already checking in?"

"Checking in? I wasn't planning to do that until tonight. This is business. We've got a problem. Jenna's gone into labor."

Opal's only other full-time employee, Jenna Monroe, was eight months pregnant and glowing with it. At least she had been when Chloe had seen her the previous day. "She's not due for another four weeks."

"Maybe not, but the baby has decided to make an appearance. You're going to have to handle the setup for the Morran wedding on your own until I can get there."

"I'll call Mary Alice—"

"Mary Alice is going to have to stay at the store. We can't afford to close for the day and between the two of you, she's the better floral designer."

"It doesn't take much to be better than me." Chloe's dry comment fell on deaf ears, Opal's voice continuing on, giving directions and listing jobs that needed to be done before the wedding guests arrived at the church.

"So, that's it. Any questions?"

"No. But you do realize I've only been working at Blooming Baskets for five days, right?"

"Are you saying you can't do this?"

"I'm saying I'll try, but I can't guarantee the results."

"No need to guarantee anything. I've already left Baltimore. I'll be in Lakeview at least an hour before the wedding. We'll finish the job together."

"If I haven't ruined everything by then."

"What's to ruin? We're talking flowers, ribbons and bows." Opal paused, and Chloe could imagine her raking a hand through salt and pepper curls, her strong face set in an impatient frown. "Look, I have faith in your ability to handle this. Why don't you try to have some, too?"

The phone clicked as Opal disconnected, and Chloe set the receiver down.

Faith? Maybe she'd had it once—in herself and her

abilities, in those she cared about. But that was before the accident, before Adam's death. Before his betrayal. Before everything had changed.

Now she wasn't even sure she knew what the word meant.

It didn't take long to shower and change, to grab her keys and make her way out of her one-bedroom apartment and into the dark hallway of the aging Victorian she lived in.

Outside it was still dark, brisk fall air dancing through the grass and rustling the dying leaves of the bushes that flanked the front porch. Chloe scanned the shadowy yard, the trees that stretched spindly arms toward the heavens, the inky water of Smith Mountain Lake. There seemed a breathless quality to the morning, a watchful waiting that crawled along Chloe's nerves and made the hair on the back of her neck stand on end. A million eyes could be watching from the woods beside the house, a hundred men could be sliding silently toward the car and she'd never know it, never see it until it was too late.

Cold sweat broke out on her brow, her hand shaking as she got in the car and shoved the keys into the ignition.

"You are not going to have a panic attack about this." She hissed the words as she drove up the long driveway and turned onto the road, refusing to think about what she was doing, refusing to dwell on the darkness that pressed against the car windows. Soon dawn would come, burning away the night and her memories. For now, she'd just have to deal with both.

Forty minutes later, Chloe arrived at Grace Christian Church, the pink Blooming Baskets van she'd picked up at the shop loaded with decorations and floral arrangements. It was just before seven. The wedding was scheduled for noon. Guests would arrive a little before then. That meant she had four hours to get ready for what Opal and Jenna had called the biggest event to take place in Lakeview in a decade. And Chloe was the one setting up for it.

She would have laughed if she weren't so sure she was about to fail. Miserably.

Cold crisp air stung her cheeks as she stepped to the back of the van and pulled open the double doors. The sickeningly sweet funeral-parlor stench nearly made her gag as she dragged the first box out.

"Need a hand?"

The voice was deep, masculine and so unexpected Chloe jumped, the box of wrought iron candelabras dropping from her hands. She whirled toward the sound, but could see nothing but the deep gray shadows of trees and foliage. "Thank you, but I'm fine."

"You sure? Looks like you've got a full van there." A figure emerged from the trees, a deeper shadow among many others, but moving closer.

"I can manage." As she spoke, she dug in her jacket pocket, her fist closing around the small canister of pepper spray she carried. She didn't know who this guy was, but if he got much closer he was going to get a face full of pain.

"I'm sure you can, but Opal won't be happy if I let you. She just ordered me out of bed and over here to help. So here I am. Ready to lend a hand. Or two." His voice was amiable, his stride unhurried. Chloe released her hold on the spray.

"Opal shouldn't have bothered you, Mr...?"

"Ben Avery. And it wasn't a bother."

She knew the name, had heard plenty about the handsome widower who pastored Grace Christian Church. Opal's description of the man's single-and-available status had led Chloe to believe he was Opal's contemporary. Late fifties or early sixties.

In the dim morning light, he looked closer to thirty and not like any pastor Chloe had ever seen, his hair just a little too long, his leather jacket more biker than preacher.

"Bother or not, I'm sure you have other things to do with your time, Pastor Avery."

"I can't think of any offhand. And call me Ben. Everyone else does." He smiled, his eyes crinkling at the corners, the scent of pine needles and soap drifting on the air as he leaned forward and grabbed the box she'd dropped.

Chloe thought about arguing, but insisting she do the job herself would only waste time she didn't have. She shrugged. "Then I guess I'll accept your help and say thanks."

"You might want to hold off on the thanks until we see how many flower arrangements I manage to massacre."

"You're not the only one who may massacre a few. I know as much about flowers as the average person knows about nuclear physics."

He laughed, the sound shivering along Chloe's nerves and bringing her senses to life. "Opal did mention that you're a new hire."

"Should I ask what else she mentioned?"

"You can, but that was about all she said. That and, 'It'll be on your head, Ben Avery, if Chloe decides to quit because of the pressure she's under today.'"

"That sounds just like her. The rat."

"She is, but she's a well-meaning rat."

"Very true." Chloe pulled out another box. "And I really could use the help. This is a big job."

"Then I guess we'd better get moving. Between the two of us we should be able to get most of the setup done before Opal arrives." Ben pushed open the church door, waiting as Chloe moved more slowly across the parking lot.

"Ladies first." He gestured for her to step inside, but Chloe hesitated.

She hated the dark. Hated the thought of what might be lurking in it. The inside of the church was definitely dark, the inky blackness lit by one tiny pinpoint of light flashing from the ceiling. She knew it must be a smoke detector, but her mind spiraled into the darkness, carried her back to the accident, to the shadowy figure standing outside the window of the car, to the eyes that had seemed to glow red, searing into her soul and promising a slow, torturous death.

She swayed, her heart racing so fast she was sure she was going to pass out.

"Hey, are you okay?" Ben wrapped a hand around her arm, anchoring her in place, his warmth chasing away some of the fear that shivered through her.

"I'm fine." Of course she *wasn't* fine. Not by a long shot. But her terror was only a feeling, the danger imagined.

She took a deep breath, stepped into the room, the darkness enveloping her as the door clicked shut. Chloe forced herself to concentrate on the moment, on the soft pad of Ben's shoes as he moved across the floor, the scent of pine needles and soap that drifted on the air around him.

Finally, overhead lights flicked on, illuminating a wide hallway. Hardwood floors, creamy walls, bulletin boards filled with announcements and pictures. The homey warmth of it drew her in and welcomed her.

Chloe turned, facing Ben, seeing him clearly for the first time, her heart leaping as she looked into the most vividly blue eyes she'd ever seen. Deep sapphire, they burned into hers, glowing with life, with energy, with an interest that made Chloe step back, the box clutched close, a flimsy barrier between herself and the man who'd done what no other had in the past year—made her want to keep looking, made her want to know more, made her wish she were the woman she'd been before Adam's death.

His gaze touched her face, the scar on her neck, the mottled flesh of her hand, but he didn't comment or ask the questions so many people felt they had the right to. "The sanctuary is through here. Let's bring these in. Then I'll make some coffee before we get the rest from the van."

Chloe followed silently, surprised by her response to Ben and not happy about it. She'd made too many mistakes with Adam, had too many regrets. There wasn't room for anything else. Or anyone.

"Where do you want these?" Ben's question pulled her from her thoughts and she glanced around the large room. Rows of pews, their dark wood gleaming in the overhead light, flanked a middle aisle. A few stairs led to a pulpit and a choir loft, a small door to one side of them closed tight.

"On the first pew will be fine. I'll start there and work my way back." She avoided looking in Ben's direction as she spoke, preferring to tell herself she'd imagined the bright blue of his eyes, the warm interest there. He was a pastor, after all, and she was a woman who had no interest in men.

"Am I making you nervous?"

Startled, Chloe glanced up, found herself pulled into his gaze again.

"No." At least not much. "Why do you ask?"

"Sometimes my job makes people uncomfortable." He smiled, his sandy hair and strong, handsome face giving him a boy-next-door appearance that seemed at odds with the intensity in his eyes.

"Not me." Though *Ben* seemed to be having that effect on her.

"Good to know." He smiled again, but his gaze speared into hers and she wondered what he was seeing as he looked so deeply into her eyes. "And just so we're clear. Florists don't make *me* uncomfortable."

Despite herself, Chloe smiled. "Then I guess that means we'll both be nice and relaxed while we work."

"Not until we have some coffee. I don't know about you, but I'm not much good for anything until I've had a cup."

His words were the perfect excuse to end the conversation and move away from Ben, and Chloe started back toward the sanctuary door, anxious to refocus her thinking, recenter her thoughts. "I'll keep unloading while you make some."

Ben put a hand on her shoulder, stopping her before she could exit the room. "If the rest of the boxes are as heavy as the last one, maybe you should make the coffee and I should unload."

"I'll be fine."

"*You* will be, but I won't if Opal finds out I let you carry in a bunch of heavy boxes while I made coffee."

"Who's going to tell her?"

"I'd feel obligated to. After all, she's bound to ask how things went and I'm bound to tell the truth."

For the second time since she'd met Ben, Chloe found herself smiling at his words. Not good. Not good at all. Men were bad news. At least all the men in Chloe's life had been. The sooner she put distance between herself and Ben, the better she'd feel. "Since you put it that way, I guess I can't argue."

"Glad to hear it, because arguing isn't getting me any closer to having that cup of coffee. Come on, I'll show you to the kitchen." He strode out of the sanctuary, moving with long, purposeful strides.

Chloe followed more slowly, not sure what it was about Ben that had sparked her interest and made her want to look closer. He was a man, just like any other man she'd ever known, but there was something in his eyes—secrets, depths—that begged exploration.

Fortunately, she'd learned her lesson about men the hard way and she had no intention of learning any more. She'd just get through the wedding preparations, get through the day, then go back to her apartment and forget Ben Avery and his compelling gaze.

TWO

The industrial-size kitchen had a modern feel with a touch of old-time charm, the stainless steel counters and appliances balanced by mellow gold paint, white cabinets and hardwood floor. Chloe hovered in the doorway, wary, unsure of herself in a way she hadn't been a year ago, watching as Ben plugged in a coffeemaker and pulled a can of coffee from a cupboard. He gestured her over and Chloe stepped into the room ignoring the erratic beat of her heart. "This is a nice space."

"Yeah, it is, but I can't take credit. We remodeled a couple of years ago. The church ladies decided on the setup and color scheme. Opal pretty much spearheaded the project."

"That doesn't surprise me. She's a take-charge kind of person. It's one of the things I admire about her."

"Have you known her long?" He leaned a hip against the counter, relaxed and at ease. Apparently not at all disturbed by the fact that he'd been called out of bed before dawn on a cool November day to help a woman he didn't know set up flowers for a wedding he was probably officiating.

Strange.

Interesting.

Intriguing.

Enough!

Chloe rubbed the scarred flesh on her wrist, forcing her thoughts back to the conversation. "Since I was a kid."

"You grew up in Lakeview?" His gaze was disconcerting, and Chloe resisted the urge to look away.

"No, I visited in the summer." She didn't add more. The past was something she didn't share. Especially not with strangers.

Ben seemed to take the hint, turning away and pulling sugar packets from a cupboard. "It's a good place to spend the summer. And the fall, winter and spring." He smiled. "There's cream in the fridge if you take it. I'd better get moving on those boxes."

With that he strode from the room, his movements lithe and silent, almost catlike in their grace. He might be a pastor now, but Chloe had a feeling he'd been something else before he'd felt a call to ministry. Military. Police. Firefighter. Something that required control, discipline and strength.

Not that it mattered or was any of her business.

Chloe shook her head, reaching for a coffee filter and doing her best to concentrate on the task at hand. Obviously, the nightmare had thrown her off, destroying her focus and hard-won control. She needed to get both back and she needed to do it now. Opal was counting on her. There was no way she planned to disappoint the one person in her life who had never disappointed her.

She paced across the room, staring out the window above the sink, anxiety a cold, hard knot in her chest. New beginnings. That's what she hoped for. Prayed for. But maybe she was too entrenched in the past to ever escape it. Maybe coming to Lakeview was nothing more than putting off the inevitable.

Outside, dawn bathed the churchyard in purple light and deep shadows, the effect sinister. Ominous. A thick stand of trees stood at the far end of the property, tall pines and heavy-branched oaks reaching toward the ever-brightening sky. As the coffee brewed, the rich, full scent of it filled the kitchen, bringing memories of hot summer days, lacy curtains, open windows, soft voices. Safety.

But safety and security never lasted. All Chloe could hope for was a measure of peace.

She started to turn away from the window, but something moved near the edge of the yard, a slight shifting in the darkness that caught her attention. Was that a person standing in the shadows of the trees? It was too far to see the details, the light too dim. But Chloe was sure there *was* a person there. Tall. Thin. Looking her way.

She took a step back, her pulse racing, her skin clammy and cold. This was the nightmare again. The stranger watching, waiting on the other side of the glass. Only this time Chloe wasn't trapped in a car and surrounded by flames. This time she was able to run. And that's just what she did, turning away from the window, rushing from the kitchen and slamming into a hard chest.

She flew back, her bad leg buckling, her hands searching for purchase. Her fingers sank into cool leather as strong arms wrapped around her waist and pulled her upright.

"Careful. We've got a lot to do. It's probably best if we don't kill each other before we finish." Ben's words tickled against her hair, his palms warm against her ribs. He felt solid and safe and much too comfortable.

Chloe stepped back, forcing herself to release her white-knuckled grip on his jacket. "Sorry. I didn't mean to run you down."

"You didn't even come close." His gaze swept over her, moving from her face, to her hands and back again. "Is everything okay? You look pale."

"I…" But what was she going to say? That she'd seen someone standing outside the church? That she thought it might be the same person who'd stood outside her burning car, watching while the flames grew? The same person who'd been in jail for eleven months? "Everything is fine. I'm just anxious to get started in the sanctuary."

He stared hard, as if he could see beyond her answer to the truth that she was trying to hide, the paranoia and fear that had dogged her for months. Finally, he nodded. "How about we grab the coffee and get started?"

Go back into the kitchen? Back near the window that looked out onto the yard? Maybe catch another glimpse of whoever was standing near the trees. No thanks. "You go ahead. I'll start unpacking boxes."

She hurried back toward the sanctuary, feeling the weight of Ben's gaze as she stepped through the double wide doors. She didn't look back, not wanting him to see the anxiety and frustration in her face.

She'd been so sure that moving away from D.C., leaving behind her apartment, her job, starting a new life, would free her from the anxiety that had become way too much a part of who she was. Seven days into her "new" life and she'd already sunk back into old patterns and thought processes.

Her hands trembled as she pulled chocolate-colored ribbon from a box and began decorating the first pew. Long-stemmed roses—deep red, creamy white, rusty orange—needed to be attached. She pulled a bouquet from a bucket Ben had brought in and wrestled it into place, a few petals falling near her feet as she tied a lopsided bow around the stems.

"Better be careful. Opal won't like it if the roses are bald when she gets here." Ben moved toward her, a coffee cup in each hand, sandy hair falling over his forehead.

"Hopefully, she won't notice a few missing petals."

"A few? No. A handful? Maybe." He set both cups on a pew and scooped up several silky petals. "I brought you coffee. Black. You didn't look like the sugar and cream type."

He was right, and Chloe wasn't sure she was happy about it. "What gave it away?"

"Your eyes." He didn't elaborate and Chloe didn't ask, just lifted the closest cup, inhaling the rich, sharp scent of the coffee and doing her best to avoid Ben's steady gaze.

Which annoyed her. She'd never been one to avoid trouble. Never been one to back away from a challenge. Never been. But the accident had changed her.

She took a sip of the coffee, pulled more ribbon from the box, forcing lightness to her movements and to her voice. "They say the eyes are the window to the soul. If you're seeing black coffee in mine, I'm in big trouble."

"I'm seeing a lot more than black coffee in there." He grabbed a bouquet of roses, holding it while Chloe hooked it in place and tied a ribbon around the stems, feeling the heat of Ben's body as he leaned in close to help, wondering what it was he thought he saw in her eyes.

Or maybe not wondering. Maybe she knew. Darkness. Sorrow. Guilt. Emotions she'd tried to outrun, but that refused to be left behind.

She grabbed another ribbon, another bouquet, trying to lose herself in the rhythm of the job.

"The flowers look good. Are they Opal's design, or Jenna's?" The switch in subjects was a welcome distraction, and Chloe answered quickly.

"I'm not sure. They were designed months before I started working at Blooming Baskets."

"Do you like it there?"

"Yes." She just wasn't sure how good she was at it. Digging into the bowels of a computer hard drive to find hidden files was one thing. Unraveling yards of tulle and ribbon and handling delicate flowers was another. "But it's a lot different than what I used to do."

"What was that?"

"Computers." She kept the answer short. Giving a name to her job as a computer forensic specialist usually meant answering a million questions about her chosen career.

Former career.

"Sounds interesting."

"It was." It had also been dangerous. Much more dangerous than she ever could have imagined before Adam's death. But that was something she didn't need to be thinking about when she had a few dozen pews and an entire reception hall left to decorate.

Chloe pulled out more ribbon, started on the next pew and wondered how long it was going to take to complete the decorations on the rest. Too long. Unless she started working a lot faster.

She moved forward, more ribbon in her hand. Ben moved with her, his sandy head bent close to hers as he helped hold the next bunch of roses in place, his presence much more of a distraction than it should have been. "Maybe we should split up. You take the pews on the other side of the aisle. I'll finish the ones over here."

"Trying to get rid of me?"

Absolutely. "I just think we'll get the job done more quickly that way."

"Maybe, but we seem to be making pretty good headway together. Two sets of hands are definitely helpful in this kind of work."

He had a point. A good one. If she had to hold the flowers *and* tie the ribbons it would probably take double the time. And time was not something she had enough of. "You're probably right. Let's keep going the way we are."

"Silently?"

Chloe glanced up into Ben's eyes, saw amusement there. "I don't mind talking while we work."

"As long as it's not about the past?"

"Something like that."

"I bet that limits conversation."

Chloe shrugged, tying the next bow, grabbing more ribbon. "There are plenty of other things to talk about."

"Like?"

"Like what Opal's going to say if she gets here and we're not done."

The deep rumble of Ben's laughter filled the air. "Point taken. I'll lay off the questions and move a little faster."

Four hours later, Chloe placed the last centerpiece on the last table in the reception hall; the low bowl with floating yellow, cream and burnt umber roses picked up the color in the standing floral arrangements that dotted the edges of the room. Roses. Lilies. A half a dozen other flowers whose names she didn't know.

"You did it! And it looks almost presentable." Opal Winchester's voice broke the silence and Chloe turned to face the woman who'd been surrogate mother to her during long-ago summers, watching as she moved across the room, her salt and pepper curls bouncing around a broad face, her sturdy figure encased in a dark suit and pink shirt.

"I didn't do it alone."

"I know. Where is that good-looking young pastor?"

"Home getting ready for the wedding. Which he's officiating after spending almost four hours helping with the floral decorations."

"Did he complain?"

"No."

"Then I don't expect you to, either." Opal slid an arm around Chloe's waist and surveyed the room. "It's beautiful, isn't it?"

"It is. You and Jenna did a great job."

"So did you and Ben." Opal cast a sly look in Chloe's direction, her dark eyes sparkling. "So, what did you think of him?"

"Who?"

"Ben Avery. As if you didn't know."

"He's helpful."

"And?"

"And he's helpful." Chloe brushed thick bangs out of her eyes and limped a few steps away from Opal, smoothing a wrinkle out of a tablecloth, determined not to give her friend any hint of how Ben had effected her. "How was your drive?"

"You're changing the subject, but I'll allow it seeing as how I'm so proud of what you've accomplished this morning. The drive was slow. I thought I'd never get here." Opal adjusted a centerpiece, straightened a bow on one of the chairs. "But I'm here and happy to announce that Jenna had a bouncing baby boy fifteen minutes ago."

"That's wonderful!"

"Isn't it? A wedding and a birth on the same day. You can't ask for much better than that. I'm going to stop by the hospital after the reception is over. Maybe slip Jenna a piece of wedding cake if Miranda and Hawke don't mind me bringing her some. Speaking of which," She paused, spearing Chloe with a look that warned of trouble. "You're going to have to attend."

"Attend?"

"The wedding."

"No way." She had no intention of staying to witness the marriage of two people she didn't know, two people who, according to both Jenna and Opal, were *meant to be together*.

Meant to be.

As if such a thing were possible. As if *meant to be* didn't always turn into goodbye.

"I understand your reluctance, Chloe, but it's expected."

"You know I never do what's expected."

"I know you never did what was expected. You're starting fresh here and in a small town like Lakeview, doing what's expected is important."

"Opal—"

"Don't make me use my mother voice." She glowered, straightening to her full five-foot-three height.

"I'm not ready for a big social event."

"Well, then you'd better get ready. The entire church was invited to the ceremony and the reception. It's a community event."

"I don't attend this church."

"But Jenna does. You'll be taking her place, offering support to the couple and representing Blooming Baskets."

"I'm sure—"

"I won't listen to any more excuses. I don't like them."

The words were harsh, but Opal's expression softened, her dark eyes filled with sympathy. "It's been a year, Chloe. It's time to move on. That's why you're here. That's what you want. And it's what I want for you. So, ready or not, you're attending the wedding."

Much as Chloe wanted to argue, she couldn't deny the truth of Opal's words. She did want to leave the past behind, to focus on the present and the future. To create the kind of life she'd once thought boring and mundane but now longed for. "Okay. I'll stay. For a while."

"Good. Now, I'm going to make sure everything is perfect in the sanctuary. You grab yourself a cup of coffee and put your leg up for a while."

"I'll come with you."

"You'll do exactly what I told you to do." Opal bustled away, leaving Chloe both amused and frustrated. Opal was a force to be reckoned with. In her absence, the room felt empty, the hollow aloneness of the moment a hard knot in Chloe's chest, the beauty of the flowers, the tables, the bows and ribbons reminding her of the wedding she'd almost had.

Almost.

All her plans, all her dreams had died well before the accident. Now her dreams were much simpler and much less romantic. She wanted to forget, wanted to move on, wanted to rebuild her life. Maybe with God's help she could do that, though even here in His house, she felt He was too far away to see her troubles, too far away to care.

And that, more than the flowers and decorations and memories, made her feel truly alone.

THREE

Ben Avery's attention should have been on the bride and groom, the wedding party, the guests who joked and laughed, ate and talked as the reception wound its way through hour three with no sign of slowing. Instead, his gaze was drawn again and again to Chloe Davidson. Straight black hair gleaming in the overhead light, slim figure encased in a fitted black pantsuit, she smiled and chatted as she moved through the throng, her limp barely noticeable. On the surface, she seemed at ease and relaxed, but there was a tension to her, a humming energy that hadn't ebbed since he'd first seen her unloading the van.

He watched as she approached Opal Winchester, said a few words, then started toward the door that led outside. Maybe she needed some air, a few minutes away from the crowd, some time to herself. And maybe he should leave her to it. But he'd seen sadness in her eyes and sensed a loneliness that he knew only too well.

And he was curious.

He admitted it to himself as he smiled and waved his way across the reception hall and out the door. Already the day was waning, the sky graying as the sun began its slow descent. The air felt crisp and clean, the quiet sounds of rural life a music that Ben never tired of hearing.

He glanced around the parking lot, saw Chloe leaning against Blooming Baskets' pink van and strode toward her. "It looks like the flowers were a big success."

"Opal is pleased, anyway." Her eyes were emerald-green and striking against the kind of flawless skin that could have graced magazine covers. Only a deep scar on the side of her neck marred its perfection.

"She should be. You worked hard." He leaned a shoulder against the van, studying Chloe's face, wondering at the tension in her. Opal had told him almost nothing about the woman she'd hired a week ago. Only that Chloe was recovering from surgery and working at Blooming Baskets. There was more to the story, of course. A lot more. But Ben doubted he'd get answers from either woman.

"So did you. Thanks again for all your help." She smiled, but the sadness in her eyes remained.

"It was no problem. People in my congregation call me all the time for help." Though he had to admit he'd been surprised by Opal's early morning summons. Flowers? Definitely not his thing.

"That may be true, but being woken up before dawn and asked to do a job you're not getting paid for goes way beyond the call of duty."

"But not beyond the call of friendship."

"If that's the case, Opal is lucky to have a friend like you."

"In my experience, luck doesn't have a whole lot to do with how things work out."

"You're right about that." She straightened, brushing thick black bangs from her eyes. "Opal came into my life just when I most needed someone. I've always thought that was a God thing. Not a luck thing."

"But?"

She raised an eyebrow at his question, but answered it. "Lately it's been hard to see much of God in the things that have happened in my life."

"You've had a hard time." The scars on her neck and hand were testimony to that, the pain in her eyes echoing the physical evidence left by whatever had happened.

Chloe's gaze was focused on some distant point. Maybe the trees. Maybe the last rays of the dying sun. Maybe some dream or hope that had been lost. "Yes, but things are better now."

He was sure he heard a hint of doubt in her voice, but she didn't give him a chance to comment, just shrugged too-thin shoulders. "I'd better get back inside before Opal sends out a posse."

The words and her posture told Ben the conversation was closed. He didn't push to open it again. Much as he might be curious about Chloe, he had no right to press for answers. "I'm surprised she hasn't already. There must be at least five unmarried men she hasn't introduced you to yet."

"Is that what was going on? I was wondering why almost every person she introduced me to was male." She laughed, light and easy, her body losing some of its tension, her lips curving into a full-out grin that lit her face, glowed in her eyes.

"You should do that more often."

The laughter faded, but the smile remained. "Do what?"

"Smile."

"I've been smiling all day."

"Your lips might have been, but your heart wasn't in it."

She blinked, started to respond, but the door to the reception hall flew open, spilling light and sound out into the deepening twilight.

"There you are!" Opal's voice carried over the rumble of wedding excitement as she hurried toward them. "Things are winding down. It won't be long before Hawke and Miranda leave."

"Are you hinting that we should get back inside?"

"You know me better than that, Ben. I never hint."

It was true. In the years Ben had been pastoring Grace Christian Church, Opal had never hesitated to give her opinion or state her mind. A widow who'd lost her husband the same year Ben lost his wife, she was the one woman Ben knew who'd never tried to set him up with a friend, relative or acquaintance.

She had, however, told him over and over again that a good pastor needed a good wife. Maybe she was right, but Ben wasn't looking for one. "So, you're *telling* us we should get back inside?"

"Exactly." She smiled. "So, let's go."

There was no sense arguing. Ben didn't want to anyway. He'd come outside to make sure Chloe was okay and to satisfy his curiosity. He'd accomplished the first. The second would take a little more time. Maybe a lot more time.

That was something Ben didn't have.

Much as he loved his job, being a pastor was more than a full-time commitment. Opal's opinion about a pastor needing a wife aside, Ben had no room for anything more in his life. That was why he planned to put Chloe Davidson and her sad-eyed smile out of his mind.

Planned to.

But he knew enough about life, enough about God, to

know that his plans might not be the best ones. That sometimes things he thought were too much effort, too much time, too much commitment, were exactly what God wanted. Only time would tell if Chloe was one of those things.

He pushed open the reception hall door, allowing Chloe and Opal to step in ahead of him. Light, music, laughter and chatter washed over him, the happy excitement of those in attendance wrapping around his heart and pulling him in.

"Ben!" Hawke Morran stepped toward him, dark hair pulled back from his face, his scar a pale line against tan skin.

Ben grabbed his hand and shook it. "Things went well."

"Of course they did. I was marrying Miranda. Thank you for doing the ceremony. And for everything else. Without your help we might not be here at all." The cadence to his words, the accent that tinged them, was a reminder of where he'd grown up, of the life he'd lived before he'd come to the States to work for the DEA, before he'd been set up and almost killed. Ben had met him while he was on the run, offered the help Hawke needed, and forged a friendship with him.

"There's no need to thank me. I was glad to help."

"And I'm glad to have made a friend during a very dark time." He smiled, his pale gaze focused on his wife.

"Are you returning to Thailand for your honeymoon?"

"We are. I want Miranda to experience it when she's not running for her life."

"Try to stay out of trouble this time."

"I think my days of finding trouble are over." He paused, glanced at the hoard of women who had converged on his bride. "Miranda is finally going to toss the flowers. Come on, let's get closer. My wife doesn't know it, yet, but as soon as she finishes, she's going to be kidnapped."

That sounded too good to miss and Ben followed along as Hawke moved toward the group. Miranda smiled at the women crowded in front of her, turned and tossed the bouquet. Squeals of excitement followed as the ladies jostled for position, the flowers flying over grasping hands and leaping bridesmaids before slapping into the chest of the only silent, motionless woman there.

Chloe.

Her hands grasped the flowers, pulled them in. Then, as if she realized what she was doing and didn't like it, she frowned, tossing the bouquet back into the fray. More squeals followed, more grasping and clawing for possession. Chloe remained apart from it all, watching, but not really seeming to see. Ben took a step toward her, hesitated, told himself he should let her be, then ignored his own advice and crossed the space between them.

FOUR

"I think that's the first time I've ever seen a woman catch the bouquet and throw it back." Ben Avery's laughter rumbled close to Chloe's ear, pulling her from thoughts she was better off not dwelling on. Hopes, dreams, promises. All shattered and broken.

She turned to face him, glad for the distraction, though she wasn't sure she should be. "I didn't *throw* it. I tossed it."

"Like it was a poisonous snake." The laughter was still in his voice and, despite the warning that shouted through her mind every time she was with Ben, Chloe smiled.

"More like it was a bouquet I had no use for." She glanced away from his steady gaze, watching as a little flower girl emerged triumphant from the crowd of wannabe brides, the bouquet clutched in her fist. "Besides, it seems to have gone to the right person."

Ben followed the direction of her gaze and nodded. "You may be right about that, but tell me, since when do flowers have to be useful? Aren't they simply meant to be enjoyed?"

"I suppose. But I'm not into frivolous things." Or things that reminded her of what she'd almost had. That was more to the point, but she wasn't going to say as much to Ben.

"Interesting."

"What?"

"You're not into frivolous things but you work in a flower shop." His gaze was back on Chloe, his eyes seeming to see much more than she wanted.

To Chloe's relief, a high-pitched shriek and excited laughter interrupted the conversation.

"Look," Ben cupped her shoulder, urging her to turn. "Hawke told me he was going to kidnap his bride. I wasn't sure he'd go through with it."

But he had, the broad-shouldered, hard-faced groom, striding toward the exit with his bride in his arms, the love between the two palpable. Chloe's chest tightened, her eyes burning. At least these two had found what they were seeking. At least one couple would have their happy ending.

For tonight anyway.

The cynical thought weaseled its way into Chloe's mind, chasing away the softer emotions she'd been feeling. She brushed back bangs that needed a trim and stepped away from Ben, ready to make her escape. "I'm going to start cleaning things up in the sanctuary."

"You most certainly are not." Opal appeared at her side, a scowl pulling at the corners of her mouth. "You're going home. I'll take care of things here."

"I'm not going to leave you to do all this alone."

"Who said I'd be alone?" As she spoke a white-haired gentleman stepped up beside Opal, his hand resting on her lower back. Opal glanced back and met his eyes, then turned to Chloe. "This is Sam. He and I go back a few years."

"A few decades, but she won't admit it." The older man smiled, his face creased into lines that reflected a happy, well-lived life. "Sam Riley. And you're, Chloe. I've heard a good bit about you."

"Hopefully only good things." Sam Riley? It was a name she hadn't heard before. That, more than anything, made her wonder just what kind of relationship he had with Opal.

"Mostly good things." He winked, his tan, lined face filled with humor. "But I promise not to share any of the not-so-good things I heard if you'll convince Opal to go for a walk with me after this shindig."

"Sam Riley! That's blackmail." Opal's voice mixed with Ben's laughter, her scowl matched by his smile.

"Whatever works, doll."

"How many times do I have to tell you not to call me that?" But it was obvious she didn't really mind; obvious there was something between the two. A past. Maybe even a future.

And no one deserved that more than Opal. "If you agree to go for a walk with Sam, I'll agree to go home without an argument."

Opal speared her with a look that would have wilted her when she was a scared ten-year-old spending the night with her grandmother's neighbor. "And that's blackmail, too. I thought I'd taught you'd better than that, young lady."

"You tried."

Opal looked like she was going to argue more, then her gaze shifted from Chloe to Ben and back again. She smiled, a speculative look in her dark eyes. "Of course, I'll need the van and you'll need a ride back to the shop. Ben, you don't mind giving Chloe a ride to Blooming Baskets, do you?"

"Of course not."

"I appreciate that, Ben, but we've put you out enough." It was a desperate bid to gain control of the situation. One Chloe knew was destined to fail.

"You're not putting me out at all."

"Good." Opal smiled triumphantly. "It's all settled.

We'd better get started, Sam. It's getting colder every minute and I don't plan on freezing just so you and I can go for a walk." She grabbed Sam's arm and pulled him away.

"I guess we've got our orders." Ben's hands were shoved into the pockets of his dark slacks, his profile all clean lines and chiseled angles. He would have fit just fine on the cover of *GQ*, his sandy hair rumpled, his strong features and easy smile enough to make any woman's heart jump.

Any woman except for Chloe.

Her heart-jumping, pulse-pounding days of infatuation were over. Adam's betrayal had ensured that. Still, if she'd had her camera in hand, she might have been tempted to shoot a picture, capture Ben's rugged good looks on film.

"Trying to think of a way out of this?" Ben's words drew her from her thoughts. She shook her head, her cheeks heating.

"Just wishing Opal hadn't asked you to give me a ride. Like I said, you've already done enough."

"Why don't you let me be the judge of that?" His hand closed around her elbow, the warmth of his palm sinking through the heavy fabric of her jacket as he smiled down into her eyes.

And her traitorous, hadn't-learned-its-lesson heart skipped a beat.

She wanted to pull away, but knew that would only call attention to her discomfort, so she allowed herself to be led out into the cool fall night and across the parking lot toward the trees that edged the property. Evergreens, oaks and shadows shifted and changed as Chloe and Ben moved closer. Was there someone watching? Maybe the same someone she'd seen that morning.

Chloe tensed, the blackness of the evening pressing in around her and stealing her breath. "Where's your car?"

"It's at my place. Just through these trees."

Just through the trees.

As if walking through the woods at night was nothing. As if there weren't a million hiding places in the dense foliage, a hundred dangers that could be concealed there. Chloe tried to pick up the pace, but her throbbing leg protested, her feet tangling in thick undergrowth. She tripped, stumbling forward.

Ben tightened his hold on her elbow, pulling her back and holding her steady as she regained her balance, his warmth, his strength seeping into her and easing the terror that clawed at her throat. "Careful. There are a lot of roots and tree stumps through here."

"It's hard to be careful when I can't see a thing."

"Don't worry. I can see well enough for both of us." His voice was confident, his hand firm on her arm as he strode through the darkness, and for a moment Chloe allowed herself to believe she was safe, that the nightmare she'd lived was really over.

Seconds later, they were out of the woods, crossing a wide yard and heading toward a small ranch-style house. "Here we are. Home sweet home."

"It's cute."

"That's what people keep telling me."

"You don't think so?"

"Cute isn't my forte, but my wife, Theresa, probably would have enjoyed hearing the word over and over again. Unfortunately, she passed away a year before I finished seminary and never got a chance to see the place."

"I'm sorry."

"Me, too."

"You must miss her."

"I do. She had cystic fibrosis and was really sick at the end. I knew I had to let her go, but it was still the hardest thing I've ever done."

Chloe understood that. Despite anger and bitterness over Adam's unfaithfulness, she still mourned his loss, and desperately wished she could have saved him. She imagined that years from now she'd feel the same, grieving his death and all that might have been. "I understand."

"You've lost someone close to you?" He pulled the car door open, and gestured for her to get in, his gaze probing hers.

"My fiancé." Ex-fiancé, but Chloe didn't say as much. "He died eleven months ago."

"Then I guess you do know." He waited until she slid into the car, then shut the door and walked around to the driver's side. "Had you known each other long?"

"Three years. We were supposed to be married this past June." But things had gone horribly wrong even before the accident and they'd cancelled the wedding a month before Adam's death.

"Then today's wedding must have been tough."

Chloe shrugged, not wanting to acknowledge even to herself just how tough it had been. Dreams. Hopes. Promises. The day had been built on the fairy tale of happily-ever-after and watching it unfold had made Chloe long for what she knew was only an illusion. "Not as hard as it would have been a few months ago."

"That's the thing about time. It doesn't heal the wounds, but it does make them easier to bear." He smiled into her eyes before he started the car's engine, the curve of his lips, the electricity in his gaze, doing exactly what Chloe didn't want it to—making her heart jump and her pulse leap, whispering that if she wasn't careful she'd end up being hurt again.

FIVE

It was close to seven when Chloe pulled her Mustang up to the Victorian that housed her apartment. Built on a hill, it offered a view of water and mountains, sky and grassland, the wide front porch and tall, gabled windows perfect for taking in the scenery. When Opal had brought her to look at the place the previous week, Chloe had been intrigued by the exterior. Walking through the cheery one-bedroom apartment Opal's friend had been renting out, seeing its hardwood floors and Victorian trim, modern kitchen and old-fashioned claw-foot tub, had sealed the deal. She knew she wanted to live there.

Unlike so many other places she'd lived in, this one felt like home.

Tonight though, it looked sinister. The windows dark, the lonely glow of the porch light doing nothing to chase away the blackness. Her car was the only one in the long driveway and Chloe's gaze traveled the length of the house, the edges of the yard, the stands of trees and clumps of bushes, searching for signs of danger. There were none, but that didn't make her feel better. She knew just how quickly quiet could turn to chaos, safety to danger.

She also knew she couldn't stay in the car waiting for one of the other tenants to return home or for daylight to come.

She stepped out of the car, jogging toward the house, her pulse racing as something slithered in the darkness to her right. A squirrel searching for fall harvest? A deer hoping for still-green foliage?

Or something worse?

Her heart slammed against her ribs as she took the porch steps two at a time. The front door was unlocked, left that way by one of the other tenants, and Chloe shoved it open, stumbling across the threshold and into the foyer, the hair on the back of her neck standing on end, her nerves screaming a warning.

Shut the door. Turn the lock. Get in the apartment.

The lock turned under her trembling fingers, her bad leg nearly buckling as she ran up the stairs to her apartment. She shoved the key into the lock, swung the door open. Slammed it shut again.

Safe.

Her heart slowed. Her gasping terror-filled breaths eased. Everything was fine. There was nothing outside that she needed to fear. Even if there was, she was locked in the house, locked in her apartment.

A loud bang sounded from somewhere below, and Chloe jumped, her fear back and clawing up her throat.

The back door.

The realization hit as the step at the bottom of the stairs creaked, the telltale sound sending Chloe across the room. She grabbed the phone, dialed 911, her heart racing so fast it felt as though it would burst from her chest.

Blackness threatened, panic stealing her breath and her oxygen, but Chloe refused to let it have her, forcing herself to breath deeply. To take action.

She grabbed a butcher knife from the kitchen, her gaze

on the door, her eyes widening with horror as the old-fashioned glass knob began to turn.

Chloe clutched the phone in one hand and the knife in the other, praying the lock would hold and wondering if passing out might be better than facing whatever was on the other side of the door.

Ben Avery bounced a redheaded toddler on his knee, and smiled at his friend, Sheriff Jake Reed, who was cradling a dark-haired infant. "I'm thinking we may be able to go fishing again in twenty-one years."

"You're going next weekend." Tiffany Reed strode into the room, her red hair falling around her shoulders in wild waves. Three weeks after having her second child, she looked as vivacious and lovely as ever. "Jake needs a break."

"From what?" Jake stood, laid the baby in a bassinet and wrapped his arms around his wife. "This is where I want to be."

"I know that, but Ben's made two week's worth of meals for us. It's time for you to take him out to thank him."

Ben stood, the little girl in his arms giggling as he tickled her belly. "I made the meals because I wanted to. I don't need any thanks."

"Of course you don't, but you and Jake are still going fishing next weekend. Right, honey?"

Jake met Ben's eyes, shrugged and smiled. "I guess we are. What time?"

Before Ben could reply, Jake's cell phone rang. He glanced at the number. "Work. I'd better take it."

Tiffany pulled her daughter from Ben's arms, shushing the still-giggling child and carrying her from the room.

Ben made himself comfortable, settling back onto the

sofa and waiting while Jake answered the phone. Whatever was happening couldn't be good if Jake was being called in.

"Reed here. Right. Give me the address." He jotted something down on a piece of paper. "Davidson?"

At the name, Ben straightened, an image of straight black hair and emerald eyes flashing through his mind.

"Okay. Keep her on the phone. I'll be there in ten." Jake hung up, grabbed a jacket from the closet.

"You said Davidson?"

"Yeah. Lady living out on the lake in the Richard's place is reporting an intruder in the house. My men are tied up at an accident outside of town, so I'm going to take the call."

"Did you get a first name?"

"Chloe."

"I'm coming with you."

Jake raised an eyebrow. "Sorry, that's not the way it works."

"It is this time. I'll stay in the squad car until you clear things, but I'm coming."

"Since I don't have time to argue or ask questions, we'll do it your way."

It took only seconds for Jake to say goodbye to his family, but those seconds seemed like a lifetime to Ben, every one of them another opportunity for whoever was in the house with Chloe to harm her. As they climbed into the cruiser and sped toward the lake, Ben could only pray that she'd be safe until he and Jake arrived.

Sirens sounded in the distance and Chloe backed toward the window that overlooked the front door, her gaze still fixed on the glass knob. It hadn't turned again, but she was expecting it to and wondering what she'd do if or when the door crashed open.

"Chloe? Are you still there?" The woman on the other end of the line sounded as scared as Chloe felt.

"Yes." She glanced out the window, saw a police cruiser pull up to the house, lights flashing, sirens blaring. "The police are here. I'm going to hang up."

"Don't—"

But Chloe was already disconnecting, tossing the phone and knife onto the couch and hurrying toward the door. The stairs creaked, footsteps pounded on wooden steps and a fist slammed against the door. "Ms. Davidson? Sheriff Jake Reed. Are you okay?"

"Fine." She pulled the door open, stepping back as a tall, hard-faced man strode in, a gun in his hand.

"Good. I'm going to escort you to my car. I want you to stay there until I'm finished in here."

"Finished?"

"Making sure whoever was here isn't still hanging around."

Still hanging around?

Chloe didn't like the sound of that and hurried down the stairs and outside, the crisp fall air making her shiver. Or maybe it was fear that had her shaking.

"I won't be long. Stay in the car until I come back out. I don't want to mistake you for the intruder."

"And I don't want to be out here alone." She might not like the idea of someone being in the house, but she liked the idea of staying outside by herself even less.

"Then it's good you don't have to be." As he spoke a figure stepped out of the cruiser. Tall, broad-shouldered and moving with lithe and silent grace.

Chloe knew who it was immediately, her visceral response announcing his name, her betraying heart leaping in acknowledgement. "Ben, what are you doing here?"

"How about we discuss it in the cruiser?" He wrapped an arm around her waist and hurried her down the steps. Strong, solid, dependable in a way Adam had never been. The comparison didn't sit well with Chloe. Noticing how different Ben was from the man she'd once loved was something she shouldn't be doing.

"Climb in." He held the cruiser door open for her, then slid in himself, his knee nudging her leg, his arm brushing hers.

She scooted back against the door, doing her best to ignore the scent of pine needles and soap that drifted on the air, but he leaned in close, his jaw tight, his face much harder than it had seemed earlier. "Are you okay?"

"Just scared."

"Jake said someone was inside the house with you. Did he make it into your apartment?"

"No, but it looked like he was trying to get in." She shuddered, watching as the lights in the attic area of the Victorian flicked on.

"Did you see the person?"

"I saw something before I went in the house, but if it was a person, I couldn't tell. There was no way I was going to open the apartment door to take a look."

"I'm glad you didn't. That would have been a bad idea." The porch light flicked off, then on again, and Ben pushed open the car door. "That's Jake's all clear. Ready to go back inside?"

"Of course." But she wasn't really. Sitting in the car with Ben seemed a lot safer than stepping back into the darkness.

He rounded the car, pulled open her door and offered a hand. "It'll be okay, Chloe. Whoever it was is long gone."

Chloe nodded, not trusting herself to speak, afraid anything she said would be filled with the panic and paranoia that had chased her from D.C. Nightmares. Terror. The feeling of being watched, of being stalked. She'd been plagued with all of them since being released from the hospital nine months ago. Post-traumatic stress. That's what the doctors said. That's what the police said. Given enough time, Ben and Jake would probably say the same.

She braced herself as she stepped back into the house, sure that Jake would tell her he'd found nothing, that her mind had been playing tricks on her, that nothing had happened. She was only partially right.

Jake seemed convinced that something *had* happened, but his list of evidence was slim—an unlocked back door, a smudge of dirt on the back deck that might have been a foot-print, fingerprints that might have belonged to the intruder, but more likely belonged to someone who lived in the house.

"We'll get prints of the other tenants. See if I've picked up anything that doesn't belong to one of you. Can you come to the station Monday?"

"I've got to work, but I'm sure Opal will give me the time off."

"Good. In the meantime, keep the doors locked and don't take unnecessary risks. I'm thinking this is probably a kid playing a prank or hoping to find some quick cash, but you never know."

"No, you don't." Chloe shifted her weight, trying to ease the ache in her leg, trying to convince herself that the sheriff was right and that what had just happened had nothing to do with her former life.

Tried, but wasn't successful.

He must have sensed her misgivings. His gaze sharpened, going from warm blue to ice. "Is there something you're not telling me? If so it's best to get it out in the open now."

"I'm just not sure what happened tonight was random." There. It was out. For better or worse. If it made her look crazy, so be it.

"And you have a reason for thinking that?" His tone was calm, but there was an edge to his words, a hardness to his face that hadn't been there before.

"This isn't the first time I've been followed into a building. It's not the first time I've felt like I was in danger."

"It sounds like there's a lot more to the story than what happened tonight. Maybe we should finish this discussion in your apartment." He started up the stairs, giving Chloe no choice but to follow.

Which was fine.

It was better to get everything out on the table now rather than later. And Chloe was pretty sure there *would* be a later. As much as she'd hoped things would be different here, she hadn't been convinced she could leave all her troubles behind. Apparently, she'd been right.

"Do you want me to wait outside?" Ben spoke quietly as he followed her up the stairs and Chloe knew what her answer should be. Yes, wait outside. Yes, keep your distance.

Unfortunately, knowing what she should say didn't make her say it. "No. You're fine. I'm going to get some coffee started. Then we'll talk."

She stepped into the living room, limped to the kitchen, and pulled coffee and a package of cookies from the cupboard. If she had to talk about the past, she might as well have sugar in her while she did it.

"Cookie, anyone?"

The sheriff shook his head, a hint of impatience in his eyes. "You were going to tell me why you don't think tonight was a prank."

Chloe nodded, forcing her muscles to relax and her tone to remain calm. Sounding hysterical was a surefire way to make herself seem unbalanced. "Eleven months ago someone tried to kill me. He failed."

The words had an immediate effect. Both men straightened, leaned toward her. Intent. Focused. Concerned.

Now if they'd just stay that way through the entire story, Chloe might believe that things really were going to be different.

"Who?" Jake pulled a small notebook from his pocket, started scribbling notes in it.

"A man named Matthew Jackson."

"Do you know where he is now?"

"Federal prison serving a life sentence for murder."

"Murder?" Ben reached over and took the cookies from her hand, pulled two out of the package and handed her one.

"My fiancé was killed in the accident Jackson caused."

Jake glanced up from the notepad. "And you think that has something to do with what happened tonight?"

"I don't know. I just know that ever since the accident, things have been happening."

"Things?"

Was there a tinge of doubt in Jake's voice, a look of disbelief on his face? Or was Chloe just imagining what she'd seen so many times on the faces of so many other police officers. "Like I said, I've had the feeling that I was being followed. A couple of times I was sure someone had been in my apartment."

There was something else, too. Something that she didn't dare bring up.

"You contacted the police?"

"Yes. They investigated."

"And?"

"At first they thought I was being stalked by some of Jackson's friends. He was part of a cult that I'd helped close down a few months earlier."

"The Strangers?" Ben took another cookie from the pack.

Surprised, Chloe met his gaze, saw the interest and concern there. "Yes."

"I remember hearing about it in the news. A computer forensics specialist was investigating a cult member's death and found evidence that implicated the leader. He went to jail for money laundering, but they couldn't prove that he'd killed his follower."

"The deceased's name was Ana Benedict. She started working as an accountant for the cult's leader and was dead a few months later. Her death was ruled a suicide, but her parents didn't believe it."

"You seem to know an awful lot about it." Jake was still writing, a frown creasing his forehead.

"I worked freelance for the private investigator Ana's parents hired. They had her laptop, but there wasn't much on it. I was hired to search for deleted files and I found plenty. Ana had documented everything. The Strangers were involved in the drug trade and were laundering money through their organization. I brought the information to the FBI."

"And Jackson blamed you when the cult dispersed."

"Yes."

"You said that after the attempt on your life, you felt like you were being followed and that someone had been in your apartment. The police suspected other cult members?"

"For a while."

"And then?"

Chloe grabbed mugs and poured coffee into them. Anything to keep from facing the two men who were watching her so intently. "They decided it was all in my head."

"I see." Jake spoke quietly, but Chloe knew he didn't see at all.

She turned back around, handing a cup to each man. "Look, Sheriff Reed—"

"Call me Jake."

"Jake, there may not be evidence proving I'm being stalked, but that doesn't mean it's not happening."

"I don't think I said it wasn't." He sipped his coffee, exchanging a glance with Ben, one that excluded Chloe and conveyed a message she couldn't even begin to figure out.

"No, you didn't, but I've been told it enough times to imagine that's what you're thinking."

"What I'm thinking is that I don't know what happened in D.C. Whatever it was, it's not going to happen here." He placed his coffee cup on the counter. "I'd better head out. If you think of anything else that might be helpful, give me a call."

"I will." Chloe followed him to the door, holding it open as he stepped out and started down the stairs.

Ben held back, the concern in his eyes obvious. "Will you be okay here alone?"

"I've been living alone since I was eighteen."

"That doesn't mean you'll be okay."

"Of course I'll be okay. What other choice do I have?" She tried to smile, but knew she failed miserably.

"You could stay with Opal."

And bring whatever danger was following her into her friend's life? Chloe didn't think so. "No, I really will be fine."

Ben watched her for a moment, his gaze so intense Chloe fidgeted. Then he nodded. "All right. Keep the doors locked and be safe."

He stepped out into the hall and pulled the door shut behind him, leaving Chloe in the silent apartment.

Be safe?

She didn't even know what the word meant anymore. She sighed, grabbed a cookie from the package and collapsed onto the easy chair. Maybe she'd figure it out again. Maybe. Somehow she doubted that would be the case.

SIX

"Sounds like your friend has a big problem." Jake's comment echoed what Ben had been thinking since he'd walked out of Chloe's apartment.

"Really big."

"Unless the police in D.C. are right and the stalker is all in her head."

"She seems pretty sure about what's been going on."

"Being sure of something only means we've convinced ourselves that it's true. I don't put much stock in it." Despite the gruff words, Jake sounded pensive and Ben knew he was leaning toward Chloe's version of things.

"You seemed to believe someone was at her apartment."

"I do. I'm just not convinced it has anything to do with what happened in D.C. It could just as easily have been a kid, or someone out to steal a few bucks."

"It could have been."

"But you don't think so?"

"I think there's more to the story than Chloe is telling. I think that until we have all the information, it'll be hard to know exactly what's going on."

"Agreed. I'm going call some friends that are still on the D.C. police force and see what they have to say." He paused as he pulled into the driveway of his house. "Regardless of what they say, I'm treating this like any other investigation until I can prove it's not one."

"I didn't expect anything less."

"And I didn't expect to be as curious about you and Chloe as I am." Jake grinned, pushed open his door. "So, are you going to tell me what's going on between you two, or am I going to have to speculate?"

"I met her at the wedding today."

"And?"

"And I would have introduced the two of you if you'd been there."

"I'm almost sorry I missed it."

"Almost?"

"Tiffany isn't ready to take the baby out or leave him with a sitter yet. I'm not ready to spend my Saturday away from her."

"Who'd have thought marriage would make you into such a romantic?" Ben grinned and got out of the car. "I'd better head home. I've got to work tomorrow."

"Good avoidance technique, but I still want to know about you and Chloe."

"You've been living small-town life for too long. You're getting nosy."

"Only when it comes to my friends."

"Sorry to disappoint, but you know as much about Chloe as I do."

"I'm not interested in what you know about her. I'm wondering what you think of her."

"Right now? I think she's a nice lady who's been hurt a lot."

"Look, Ben, if you were anyone else, I'd keep my

nose out of it, but you're not, so I'm going to say what's on my mind."

"Go ahead."

"Chloe does seem like a nice lady, but I know trouble when I see it. I see it when I look at her."

"And?"

"And be careful. I don't want that trouble coming after you."

"Thanks for the worry, but I'm pretty good at taking care of myself. I'll be fine."

Jake nodded, but his jaw was tight, his expression grim. "I've got a bad feeling about this. Really bad. Watch your back."

With that he walked away, stepping into his well-lit house, into the warmth of family and home, and leaving Ben to himself and his thoughts.

Thoughts that were similar to Jake's.

Trouble did seem to be closing in on Chloe. If Ben were smart, he'd keep his distance from it and from her. Unfortunately, he didn't think that was going to be possible. Something told him that Chloe was about to become a big part of his life. He might not want the complication, might not like it, but that seemed to be where God was leading him. If that were the case, Ben would just have to hold on tight and pray the ride wasn't nearly as bumpy as he thought it was going to be.

Apparently, Chloe's intruder was big news in Lakeview, and at least half a dozen customers converged on the flower shop minutes after it opened Monday morning. Opal seemed happy about all the business, but by noon Chloe was tired of the sometimes blatant, sometimes subtle questions. How many times and how many ways could a person say "I don't know" before she went absolutely insane?

Not many more than Chloe had already said.

She pulled a dozen red carnations from the refrigerated display case, grabbed some filler and headed back to the shop's front counter, doing her best to tamp down irritation as she listened to two elderly women discuss the "incident" in loud whispers.

"Here they are, Opal." She spoke a little more forcefully than necessary, hoping to interrupt the women's conversation.

It only seemed to make them think she wanted to be *part* of it.

The taller of the two smiled at Chloe. "Those are absolutely lovely, dear. I'm impressed that you could focus on picking the perfect flowers after such a harrowing experience."

"Thank you." What else could she say? "I try to keep my mind on the job."

"But aren't you terrified?" The shorter, more rotund woman shuddered, her owl-eyed gaze filled with both fear and anticipation, as if she were hoping for a juicy tidbit of information to pass along.

"Not really." At least no more than she'd been before she'd come to Lakeview. "The sheriff assured me he'd do everything he could to find the person responsible."

Though Chloe wondered if he'd be saying the same after he talked to the police in D.C. She wasn't looking forward to the conversation they were going to have when he found out about her recent hospitalization and its supposed cause.

She refused to worry about it and tried to focus on her job instead, shoving the carnations into a vase and scowling when two stems broke.

"Keep it up and I'll be out of business in no time." Opal took the flowers and vase from her hands, smiling at the women who were watching wide-eyed and interested. "I'll finish this up. Aren't you supposed to go to the police station today?"

"Yes, but it can wait."

"You know how I feel about procrastination. It only makes more work for everyone. Go punch out and head over there. Since we don't know how long it's going to take, I think you should just take the rest of the day off."

"We've had a lot of business so far, Opal. Are you sure you want to handle the rest of the afternoon alone?"

"I handled it alone for two years before I hired help. Besides, I've hired a kid from church to come in after school until Jenna gets back. Laura's her name. She's a senior trying to save money for college. It should work out well for all of us. Now, go ahead and do what needs doing. Then go have some fun."

"Fun?" Fun was puppies and kittens, laughter and friendship. Relaxation. Fun was something Chloe wasn't even sure she knew how to do anymore.

"Yes, fun. Go shopping. Get your nails done. Better yet, go to Becky's Diner and have a slice of warm apple pie with a scoop of ice cream on it. *That's* fun."

"It does sound good." But being at home sounded better. Safe behind closed doors and locked in tight.

"But you won't do it."

"I might."

"Hmph. We'll see, I guess. Now, get out of here. I've got work to do and you're distracting me."

"Destroying flowers *and* distracting you. I don't know why you keep me on."

"Because you bring in so much business. Now, shoo."

Chloe laughed as she stepped through the doorway that led to the back of the shop.

It didn't take long to punch out and gather her jacket and purse. Outside, the day was misty and cold, the thick clouds and steely sky ominous. Several cars were parked in the employee parking lot behind the building, but Chloe was the only person there. In the watery afternoon light, the stillness seemed unnatural, the quiet, sinister, and she was sure she felt the weight of someone's stare as she hurried toward her car.

She shivered, fumbling for her keys, the feeling that she was being watched so real, so powerful, that she was sure she'd be attacked at any moment. Finally, the key slid into the lock, the door opened and she scrambled in, slamming the door shut, locking it.

Against nothing. The parking lot was still empty of life. The day still and silent.

"You're being silly and paranoid." She muttered the words as she put the car into gear. "Being afraid because an intruder is in the house is one thing. Being afraid to cross a parking lot in the middle of the day is ridiculous."

But she *was* afraid.

No amount of self-talk, no amount of rationalization could change that.

She sighed, steering her vintage Mustang toward the parking lot exit. Opal was right. She needed to do something fun, something to get her mind off the tension and anxiety she'd been feeling since Saturday night, but she hadn't had time to make friends since she'd come to Lakeview and she had no intention of going anywhere or doing anything by herself. The fact was, despite what the

D.C. police had told her, despite what her friends, doctors and psychologist had said, she couldn't shake the feeling that danger was following her. That the accident hadn't been the end of the violence against her. That eventually the past would catch up to her. And when it did, she just might not survive.

No, she definitely didn't want to go anywhere by herself, but she didn't want to go *with* someone, either. Look what had happened to Adam because he was with her when a murderer struck.

Hot tears stung her eyes, but she forced them away. Tears wouldn't help. Only answers could do that and Chloe didn't have any. She'd been living her life, doing what she thought was right, trying her best to be the person God wanted her to be. Then the rug had been pulled out from under her, the stability she'd worked so hard for destroyed. All her childhood fears had come to pass—death, heartache, pain, faceless monsters stalking her through the darkness. Now, it seemed that God was far away, that her life had taken a taken a path that He wasn't on and that no matter how hard she tried to get back on course, she couldn't. As much as she wanted to believe differently, as much as she knew that God would never abandon His children, abandoned was exactly how she felt.

Abandoned and alone, her mind filled with nightmare images and dark shadows that reflected the hollow ache of her soul.

SEVEN

By the time she finished at the police station and returned home, it had started to rain. First a quick patter of drops, then a torrential downpour that pinged against the house's tin roof and seemed to echo Chloe's mood. Outside, the clouds had turned charcoal, bubbling up from the horizon with barely contained violence.

Chloe put her mail on the kitchen table, grabbed a glass of water and opened sliding glass doors that led to the balcony off her living room. From there she could see the stark beauty of the lake as it reflected gray clouds and bare trees. Winter would arrive soon, bringing with it colder air and a starker landscape. It would be good to capture those changes on film, to hang a few new photos on the wall. The thought brightened her mood.

It had been a long time since she'd photographed anything. In the aftermath of the accident, she hadn't had the time or the inclination. Now, with surgeries and physical therapy behind her, she did. She just hadn't had any desire to.

Except once.

An image flashed through her mind—sandy hair, vivid blue eyes, a half smile designed to melt hearts.

"Enough!" She grabbed her digital camera from the top drawer of her dresser, refusing to think about Ben and determined to do what she should have months ago—regain her life. Get back into her routines. Enjoy the hobbies she'd found so much pleasure in before the accident. Maybe she couldn't go rock climbing anymore, but she could shoot pictures. And she would.

A soft tap sounded at the front door and Chloe jumped, her heart racing. She wasn't expecting company. Anyone could be out there, waiting to finish what was started almost a year ago.

She sidled along the wall, imagining bullets piercing the door and knowing just how ridiculous she was being. "Who's there?"

"Ben Avery."

"Ben?" Surprised, relieved, Chloe pulled open the door and stepped aside so he could walk in. "What are you doing here?"

"Carrying out my orders." He smiled, rain glistening in his sandy hair and beaded on his leather jacket, the scent of fall drifting into the room with him. Fall and something else. Something masculine and strong.

Chloe took a step back. "Orders?"

"Opal and I ran into each other at the diner. She asked me to bring you this." He held out a brown paper bag, and Chloe took it, catching a whiff of apples and cinnamon.

"Apple pie?"

"And ice cream. She had Doris put that in a separate container."

"Fun in a bag?"

"I guess you could call it that."

"Those are Opal's words. Not mine. She said I should

have a little fun today. I guess she wanted to make sure I did." Chloe smiled, touched by her friend's thoughtfulness, though she wasn't sure she was happy with her methods. "Thanks for bringing this over. I'm sure you had better things to do with your time."

"It seems like we had this conversation before. And I'm going to tell you the same thing now that I did then—I can't think of any." He leaned his shoulder against the wall, his vivid blue gaze steady. "Of course, bringing it here was only part of my job."

"What was the other part?"

"I'm supposed to make sure you eat it."

"Tell me you're kidding."

"I'm afraid not. She said that if you faded away to nothing she wouldn't have any reliable help at the shop."

"She's conveniently forgetting Mary Alice and the new girl she hired."

"Laura. She mentioned that she'd left her to watch the store for a few minutes and had to hurry back."

"You and Opal must have had a long conversation."

"Not too long." He didn't seem inclined to say more, and Chloe decided not to press for details. Knowing Opal, she'd said more than she should have. Eventually, she and Chloe would have to talk about that. For now, the pie smelled too good to ignore.

"Since you've been ordered to make sure I eat this, maybe we can share." She moved into the small kitchen and set her camera down, grabbing two plates from the cupboard.

"I was hoping you'd say that. I brought enough for both of us." Ben moved toward her, an easy grin curving his lips and deepening the lines near his eyes. Was he thirty? Thirty-five? Older?

She shouldn't be wondering, but was.

And that didn't make her happy.

"You knew I was going to invite you?"

"No, but I was hoping." He pulled a large plastic container from the bag, opened it up to reveal two slices of apple pie. "It's my day off. Apple pie, ice cream and interesting company seemed like a good way to spend part of it."

"What if I hadn't asked you to stay?"

"Then I would have gone home and had a couple of oatmeal cookies in front of the TV."

"No way."

"No way what?" He served the pie, scooped ice cream onto both slices.

"No way would you be sitting home in front of the television eating oatmeal cookies."

"You're right. I would have gone back to the diner and bought more pie. It's much too good to pass up. *Then* I would have gone home and watched TV." He smiled and Chloe's pulse had the nerve to leap.

"Funny, I picture you as more the outdoor type. Hiking. Camping. Boating."

"Good call, but today is too rainy for outdoor activities."

"Then I guess I'm glad I could provide you with something to do. I'm going to have to have a talk with Opal, though. She can't keep asking you to come to my rescue."

"Who says I'm rescuing you? Maybe you're rescuing me."

"From an afternoon of boredom?"

"Exactly." He smiled again and dug into the pie, his hair falling over his forehead, his broad hands making the fork look small.

Chloe resisted the urge to pick up her camera and shoot a picture, choosing instead to fork up a mouthful of pie, the flaky crust and tart apples nearly melting in her mouth. "You're right. This *is* too good to pass up. I guess I'll have to thank Opal instead of lecturing her."

"She cares a lot about you."

"And I care a lot about her."

"You said you spent summers on the lake. Is that how you two met?"

"My grandmother rented a cottage next to Opal's property."

"Your grandmother, not your mother?"

Chloe hesitated, then shrugged. "My mother preferred to leave my upbringing to other people."

"And your grandmother filled in?"

"Not really." She scooped up another bite of pie, not willing to say any more about her childhood. "How about you? Was your family the *Father Knows Best* type?"

"It was as far from that as you can get. Absent father. Drug-addicted mother. My sister and I were in foster care by the time I was thirteen."

"I'm sorry."

"Don't be. It was the best thing that ever happened to me. My mother may not have cared much about me, but God did, and He used her neglect to get me to people who did care."

"You must have been a great kid."

He paused, his fork halfway to his mouth, his eyes so blue they seemed lit from within. "I was a little hoodlum. By the time my parents stepped in I'd been in ten foster homes, a group facility, and was about to be thrown into a juvenile detention center."

"Are you kidding?"

"Not even close to kidding. My foster parents got my

case file from a social worker they knew. A few days later they came to visit me and told me I had a choice—come stay with them and straighten up my life or stay on the path I'd chosen and end up in jail or worse."

"So you decided to straighten up."

"I wish I'd made it that easy on them. The fact is, I thought Mike and Andrea were softhearted enough to be taken advantage of. I agreed to go home with them, but had no intention at all of changing my life. Fortunately, they stuck with me." He stood and put his empty plate in the sink. "I'd better get out of here. You've probably got things you need to do."

Agree. Send him on his way. Forget the story he just told and the new light it cast him in.

But Chloe had never been great at listening to advice. Even her own.

Especially not her own.

"Nothing pressing. I was just going to take some photographs."

"A florist, a computer expert *and* a photographer? What other surprises are you hiding?" Ben settled back down into his chair and Chloe could almost imagine him as a kid, sitting in one kitchen after another, searching for someone to believe in him. To love him.

"No surprises. What you see is what you get."

"Somehow I doubt that." He steepled his fingers and stared at her across the table, his gaze somber and much too knowing.

But Chloe didn't plan on sharing more about her life, her hobbies, her past or the shadows that lived in her soul. "Doubt it all you want, but it's the truth. How about you? What surprises are you hiding?"

"The fact that I cook surprises people, but it's not something I hide."

"I wouldn't have thought a widowed pastor in a small town like this would ever have to cook. Aren't the church ladies knocking on your door begging to cook you a meal?"

"They were. That's why I had to learn to cook. By the time I'd been in town a month, I had so many casseroles in my refrigerator there wasn't room for anything else. No milk. No eggs. No vegetables or fruit. Learning to cook was a matter of self-preservation."

Chloe laughed, relaxing into the moment and the conversation. Enjoying the company. The man.

"You're laughing, but it was a serious issue." His eyes gleamed with humor as he lifted Chloe's camera. "Now it's your turn."

"My turn?"

"To tell why you got into photography."

"I moved around a lot when I was a kid. Taking pictures helped me remember where I'd been." So she would know where she didn't want to go, the kind of life she didn't want to have.

"So you do landscape photography."

"And architectural. The pictures on the wall are mine." She gestured to a black-and-white photo of the White House and a colored photo of Arlington National Cemetery.

"They're good. Mind if I take a look at the ones on your camera?

"Only if I get a chance to sample your cooking." The words were out before she could stop them and Chloe regretted them immediately. "What I mean is—"

"That you'd like to have dinner with me?" His eyes dared her to accept the offer.

"I don't think that would be a good idea."

"Really? Two friends sharing a meal sounds like a great idea to me."

She should refuse. Friendship with Ben wasn't a good idea. Friendship with *anyone* wasn't a good idea. "I don't want to drag you into my troubles, Ben."

"I'm not the type of person who gets dragged anywhere I don't want to go." He leaned across the table, and squeezed her hand. "So, how about that dinner?"

Say no.

But once again Chloe ignored her own advice. "All right. A meal with a friend."

There was no harm in that.

She hoped.

Ben smiled and released her hand, turning his attention to the camera. As she watched, his smile faded, a frown creasing his brow.

"Interesting choice of subject matter." His voice was tight, his frown deepening.

"What?" She leaned toward him, curious to see what he was looking at. It had been months since she'd used the camera. There might be photographs of Adam, of the house they'd planned to buy. Of the church where they were going to be married.

But the photo wasn't of any of those things.

Bright flowers. Dark wood. Adam lying in white silk, his face almost unrecognizable.

Ben scrolled back and the same picture appeared again. And again.

Chloe gagged, shoving away from the table and stumbling backward, her mind rebelling at what she'd seen, her body trembling with it. Panic throbbed deep in the pit of her stomach, stealing her breath until she was gasping, struggling for air.

"Hey. It's okay." Ben's voice was soothing, his hands firm on her shoulder. "Chloe, you're fine. Take a deep breath."

"I can't." Blackness edged her vision, the shadowy nightmare coming closer with every shallow breath.

"Sure you can." His hands smoothed up her neck, cupped her cheeks, forcing her to look up and into eyes so blue, so clear, she thought she could lose herself in them. "You're a survivor. A couple photos can't take that away from you."

His words were warm, but she sensed the hard determination beneath them. He had no intention of letting the nightmare take her, and that, more than anything, eased the vise around Chloe's lungs.

"Right. You're right. I'm sorry."

"Don't apologize." His words were gruff, his hands still warm against her cheeks. "Tell me what's wrong."

"I didn't take those pictures."

He stared into her eyes for another minute, then nodded. "I'd better call Jake."

His hands dropped away and he strode to the phone, leaving her in the kitchen with the camera and the horrifying images.

EIGHT

"When was the last time you used the camera?" The question was the same one Jake Reed had asked fifteen times in the past ten minutes. If he were hoping for a different answer than the one she'd already given, he was going be disappointed.

Chloe's fist tightened around the coffee mug she held, but she kept her frustration in check. "I don't know. A few months before the accident."

Jake lifted the camera in gloved hands, staring at the image. "And you didn't take these photos?"

"No!" Her tone was sharper than she'd meant and she reigned in her emotions. "They're sickening."

"Sickening, but fake."

"Fake?"

"Take another look. The guy in the casket is in a different position in each photo. The 'casket' is too wide. Looks like a twin bed with pillows and white silk on top of it."

"I'll take your word for it."

"You thought it was your fiancé?"

"Yes."

"It's not. The date on the photos is September of this

year. Months after your ex-fiancé's funeral. And he was your ex-fiancé, right?"

Apparently, he'd been talking to people in D.C. What else had they told him? Chloe's hands were clammy, but she looked him straight in the eye as she answered. "Yes, but I don't think that's relevant."

"What you think is relevant doesn't matter, Chloe. What matters is finding out what's going on. The only way to do that is to get all the information available. You didn't provide me with that Saturday night."

"I provided you with what I thought was important. My relationship with Adam was complicated. We were friends before we started dating and were trying to maintain that after we broke up." He'd wanted more than that, but Chloe hadn't been able to forgive.

"You broke up because he'd been seeing another woman."

Chloe's cheeks heated, but she nodded, refusing the urge to glance at Ben. "Adam was a nice guy. He collected friends like other people collect knickknacks. A lot of those friends were women. One became a little more than just a friend."

"You're leaving out a lot of details." Jake leaned back in the kitchen chair and tapped gloved fingers against the table. "Like the fact that you did freelance work for Adam's P.I. company. That the two of you had testified at a criminal trial the day he was killed."

"I'm sure the D.C. police were glad to fill you in."

"I would have been happier if you'd been the one to do it."

"Jake, you're not dealing with a suspect here." There was a subtle warning in Ben's voice.

"And I don't want to be dealing with a body, either. Chloe needs to be open and honest. Hiding information is never a good idea."

"I wasn't hiding information. It's just hard to talk about Adam." Chloe stood and grabbed a bottle of aspirin, her hand shaking as she tried to pry open the lid.

"Here. Let me." Ben leaned in, his shoulder brushing hers, his hands gentle as he took the bottle and popped the lid. He placed two in her hand, closed her fingers over them, his palm pressing against her knuckles, the warmth of it chasing away the chill that seemed to live in her soul. "It's going to be okay."

She wasn't so sure he was right. "Maybe."

"Things *will* be okay once we find out who's after you." Jake's voice was hard, his face grim. "Can you tell me who had access to your camera."

"Anyone who visited my apartment. I usually kept it out near my workstation."

"Can you give me a list of those people?"

"Probably, but the past few months are blurry. I had surgery on my leg a month ago and the recovery was brutal. There were people in and out all the time trying to help out."

"Do the best you can. I'll also want a list of anyone who had a key to your place in D.C."

"That's a shorter list. Jordyn Winslow. James Callahan. They both worked with Adam. Morgan Gordon had the apartment next to mine. They took turns taking care of things while I was in the hospital during the months after the accident."

"Good. We'll start there." Jake pulled a pen and small notebook from his pocket, jotted the names down. "Do you know the name of the woman Adam was involved with?"

"No. He wouldn't tell me and I didn't press for the information. Maybe I really didn't want to know."

"You didn't leave a forwarding address with the police in D.C."

"There didn't seem to be any reason."

"But you did leave it with friends?"

"I left it with some of my former employers. Companies that owed me money. No one else knows where I am. I was hoping that would keep me safe. I guess I was wrong."

"Let's not jump to conclusions yet. It's possible that whoever took the photos doesn't know where you are."

"I don't believe that. I don't think you do, either."

"There's only one thing I believe. Matthew Jackson has nothing to do with what's been happening to you. The rest I plan to find out." He closed his notebook and stood. "Do you have any other cameras?"

"A Nikon."

"Is there undeveloped film in it?"

"Yes."

"Do you mind if I take that one, too?"

"Not at all." As a matter of fact, she'd rather have it out of the house than spend the next few days wondering what might be on the undeveloped film.

She limped to her room, pulled the camera from a storage box in her closet and brought it out to Jake. "Here you go. I think I used it the week before Adam and I broke up. We'd gone on a picnic to Great Falls. The day was perfect. We…" Her voice trailed off and she shook her head. "Those should be the last pictures on the roll."

"I'll develop the film, see if there's anything there that shouldn't be. In the meantime, try not to worry too much." He smiled and she was surprised by the warmth and genuine concern in his eyes.

"I appreciate it, Jake. Thanks."

"Hold off on the thanks until I figure out what's going

on." He strode to the front door and pulled it open. "I'll see you this weekend, Ben."

"Saturday, 6 a.m. Unless that's too early."

"The baby has us up at five every day. Six won't be a problem."

Jake stepped out into the hall, hovering near the top of the steps as Ben turned to Chloe.

"I've got to head out, too, but before I leave, tell me something?"

"What?"

"Do you like fish?"

"Fish?" She'd expected a question about Adam, about their relationship. His death. She hadn't expected to be asked about fish.

"Yeah, fish. Trout. Catfish."

"Sure."

"Good. That's what I'll make, then."

"Make?"

"For dinner. We had a deal. I still need to fulfill my end of the bargain."

"That's not necessary, Ben." All thoughts of a quiet dinner spent with a friend were gone, replaced by cold dread. Something terrible had followed her from D.C. Something that was determined to destroy her and anyone who got near her.

"Isn't it?" He smiled, brushing her bangs out of her eyes and tucking long strands behind her ear.

Her stomach knotted and she stepped away. Surprised. Uncomfortable.

Afraid.

For herself. For Ben.

"No. It really isn't."

"You're chickening out."

"I'm not. I'm just…" Terrified that something terrible was going to happen. Scared that she'd be hurt. That Ben would be hurt.

"Just going to have dinner with a new friend. Is that so bad?"

"I don't want to get hurt again, Ben. And I don't want you to be hurt."

"How can having dinner hurt either of us? How does Saturday night around six sound?"

He was purposely ignoring the point and Chloe frowned. "You'll be fishing with Jake that day."

"Right. Fresh fish for dinner. What could be better?" He smiled, his eyes flashing with humor and inviting her to join in.

And despite herself, despite the warnings she knew she should heed, she relaxed. "You have a lot of faith in your ability to catch fish."

"No. I've got a lot of faith in my ability to track down a meal. If I don't find it in the lake, I'll get it from the grocery store."

"Won't that be cheating?"

"Only if I try to pass it off as my own." He grinned. "Your place or mine?"

"Mine." She answered without thought, and knew she wouldn't take the word back.

"Great. See you then." He stepped out into the hall, joining Jake there.

The other man nodded at Chloe, but she couldn't miss the concern in his eyes. Obviously, he was as worried about Ben's safety as she was. "I'll be in touch, Chloe. In the meantime, don't hesitate to call if something comes up."

"I won't."

Jake hesitated, rubbing a hand against the back of his neck. "Listen, my wife is part of a quilting circle that meets at Grace Christian on Wednesday nights. Seven o'clock. They make blankets for NICU babies and little bears for kids who have to stay at Lakeview General. They'd love to have another set of hands."

"I've never quilted before." But she couldn't deny the small part of her that longed for something new, something more than flowers and bows and evenings spent alone.

"They'll teach you everything you need to know."

"I don't usually go out at night."

"Understandable, but you'll be with a large group of people. That might be better than being here alone. Think about it. Here's my home phone number. Call my wife if you've got any questions." He scribbled the number on the back page of his notebook and tore it out.

"I will, thanks."

"No problem. Now, I really do need to get out of here. You coming? Or are you planning to spend another half hour saying goodbye?" He glanced at Ben and the amusement in his eyes was unmistakable.

"Knock it off." Ben growled the words, but smiled at Chloe, waving as he and Jake started down the stairs.

Chloe closed the door on their retreating figures, shutting out the sounds of their lighthearted banter and pacing across the living room.

She'd thought the room cozy before. In the wake of Ben and Jake's departure, it seemed empty and hollow, a sad reflection of her life.

She grimaced, moving into her bedroom, flicking on the light and turning on the CD player she kept near her bed.

An upbeat modern tune filled the room, the thrumming, strumming tempo of it doing nothing to lift Chloe's mood.

"Get over yourself, Chloe. Things could be worse."

She flopped onto the bed, knowing she should get up and do something. Television. A good book. Anything that would take her mind off the loneliness that she was suddenly feeling.

Her gaze caught on the Bible lying abandoned on the bedside table. Opal had given it to her when she was twelve and she'd had it ever since. Lately, though, she hadn't spent much time reading it. She picked it up, thumbing through it, skimming some of the passages Opal had highlighted in yellow. Little by little, she was drawn into what she was reading, her loneliness slowly fading away. She might feel as if God had abandoned her, but the truth was much different. Despite the trials and troubles she'd faced, she had to hold on to that certainty, had to believe that He was there, working His perfect will for her life. Had to trust that in the end everything would turn out okay.

But would it?

As much as she wanted to believe, to trust, Chloe couldn't imagine things getting better. She could only imagine them getting much, much worse.

She shook her head, closing the Bible, setting it back on the table and praying that she was wrong. That somehow everything *would* be okay. That what she imagined wasn't what would be and that eventually the nightmare would be over and she'd be able to rebuild her life.

NINE

Maybe quilting wasn't such a good idea after all.

Chloe stood in the doorway of the reception hall and eyed the people gathered there. Old and young, tall and short, thin and stout, they were a swarm of bees, humming with energy as they performed a dance that had meaning only to them.

She took a step back, pretty sure she'd made a poor decision when she'd left Blooming Baskets and headed toward Grace Christian. She'd come on a lark, another night alone at the apartment appealing to her about as much as a root canal. Now she was thinking a root canal might not be so bad.

"You must be Chloe." A tall redhead stepped from the throng, a broad smile creasing her face.

"That's right."

"I'm Tiffany Reed. My husband told me he'd invited you. I wanted to call and tell you a little more about what we're doing here, but Jake refused to give me your number. He said you might not be ready to face the Lakeview Quilters."

"He might have been right."

Tiffany laughed, the sound full and unapologetic. "We're not as scary as we look. Come on. I'll introduce you to a few of the ladies. Then you can get started."

"I've never quilted before in my life. I barely know how to sew."

"Not a problem. We've got people doing everything from cutting squares to stuffing bears."

"I might be able to handle that."

"Of course you can. Jake tells me you're a computer forensics specialist." She started toward the group and Chloe followed, moving fast to keep up.

"I *was* one. Now I'm a florist." Though if she smashed one more of Opal's intricate bows, she might not be that for long.

"You and I have a lot in common, then. I was a computer tech before I opened my quilt shop. I'd love to hear more about your old job. Why don't you come over after work one day? We can have a cup of coffee and chat. Of course, you'd be exposed to my noisy munchkins, so…" She blushed. "Sorry, I'm speed-talking again. I've got a two-year-old and a newborn at home. When I talk to adults, I'm so excited to actually have people that understand me, I feel like I've got to get it all out at once."

"Talking fast is better than talking to yourself. Which is what I've been doing lately."

Tiffany laughed again, looping an arm through Chloe's. "You know. I think you and I are going to get along fine. Now, let's get to work before Irma Jefferson sees us chatting and cracks the whip."

"She's the group leader?"

"No, she just thinks she is."

Chloe laughed and allowed herself to be tugged deeper into the buzz of activity.

Ben typed a sentence. Deleted it. Typed another one. Deleted *it*.

Disgusted with his lack of focus, he stood and walked

to the small window that looked out over the churchyard. Fall had ripped the leaves from the tall oak that stood in the center of the lawn. Its broad branches were clearly visible in the moonlight. Beyond that, the parking lot was still half full. Wednesday night's prayer meeting was over, but there were plenty of other activities. Choir. Youth Bible study. The quilting circle.

The quilting circle where Chloe might be.

He'd thought about calling her several times during the past few days, but had decided against it. They'd have dinner Saturday night and catch up then. Anything else seemed like…

Exactly what it was. Interest.

Ben ran a hand over his hair, rubbed the tension at the back of his neck. There were fifteen single women at Grace Christian Church. All of them were nice, sweet and as uncomplicated as women could be. Which was much more complicated than Ben wanted to deal with. Friends and acquaintances had set him up with dozens of their female relatives during the past six years— daughters, nieces, cousins, aunts. Mothers. None of them had caught and held his attention the way Chloe seemed to be doing.

He wasn't quite sure how he felt about that and was even less sure that how he felt mattered. Chloe seemed to be the direction his life was heading. Whether or not that was a good thing remained to be seen.

"Busy?" Jake's deep voice pulled Ben from his thoughts and he turned to face his friend who stood in the doorway of the office.

"No. Come on in." He waited while Jake stepped across

the threshold and closed the door. "I'm surprised to see you here. I thought you'd be on child-care duty."

"I got called into work. Tiffany's mom is babysitting the kids."

"Anything serious going on?"

"Kyle Davis is feuding with his neighbor again, insisting Jesse Rivers is stealing mail from his box."

"That does sound serious." Ben grinned, gestured to the chair across the desk. "Want to have a seat?"

"I've only got a minute. I just wanted to check in on Tiffany, make sure she's not overdoing it."

"Is it possible to overdo it while quilting?" Ben tried not to smile but failed. The gruff, hardened police officer who'd come to Lakeview five years before had definitely been softened by love.

Jake scowled. "Go ahead and laugh, my friend, but from my vantage point, it seems your time has come."

"Does it?" Ben lifted a pen from the desk, tapped it against his palm.

"You brought Chloe pie."

"Opal insisted."

"I've seen you refuse other insistent matchmakers."

True, and Ben didn't deny it. "Chloe's had a tough time."

"And is still having one." There was tightness to Jake's voice that Ben didn't like.

"You've got more information?"

"I spoke to someone else on the D.C. police force. He was willing to tell me a little more than just what's in the records."

"Like what?"

"Chloe was diagnosed with post-traumatic stress disorder a couple of months after the accident."

"And?"

"The complaints she filed were vague—things being moved around in her apartment, someone following her. She reported her laptop stolen. Then found it in the trunk of her car."

"So, they assumed she was making it up?"

"No. Both men I spoke to have worked with Chloe in the past. Her skills in computer forensics have helped close some difficult cases. Both said she was professional, intelligent, easy to work with. Neither thinks she was making things up."

"Then what do they think?"

"That losing her fiancé in an accident that was meant to take her life left her… unbalanced."

"She doesn't seem unbalanced to me. Just scared."

"I told the guy I was talking to today the same thing. He disagrees. The brake line on Chloe's car had been cut. She was driving. After the accident she told several people that she wished she'd died instead of Adam." Jake raked a hand through his hair, ran it down over his jaw. "Look, I don't know if this is something I should be sharing, but I can trust you to keep it quiet and you might have better luck getting more information about it from Chloe than I will."

"What?"

"Chloe attempted suicide two weeks before she left D.C."

Ben stilled at the words, his fist tightening around the pen he held. "No way."

"She refused to admit it, but paramedics found an empty bottle of antidepressants in her trash can. The prescription was filled less than a week before."

"Chloe called for help?"

"No. A friend called to see how Chloe was feeling and thought she sounded odd. She called an ambulance. That saved Chloe's life."

"Was the friend Opal?"

"I didn't ask, but it's possible. Chloe left D.C. less than two weeks later. Didn't bother leaving a forwarding address or telling the police that she was going. According to the guy I talked to today, Chloe insisted someone had tried to murder her. Investigation revealed nothing. No sign of forced entry into the apartment. No fingerprints but Chloe's."

"And your thoughts on this?"

"The same as they were before—I think there are missing pieces to the puzzle. I think something is going on that we don't understand. I also think I could be wrong, that maybe I'm misreading Chloe and she really does have some deep-seated problems."

Ben nodded. "I can see that."

"But you don't agree?"

"No. I don't. Chloe doesn't seem depressed enough to try and end her life."

"Maybe she isn't anymore."

"That kind of depression doesn't just go away, Jake." He dropped the pen back onto the table, rolled his shoulders trying to ease the tension in his neck. "What's the next step?"

"One of us needs to ask Chloe what happened that night."

"You're the police officer."

"I can't see upsetting the woman and that's probably what my blunt questions would do."

"You're not that bad.

"Sure I am. Even my wife says so. Speaking of which," He smiled, frustration and worry draining from his face. "I've got a redhead to track down before I go home."

"I'll walk with you, see if Chloe showed up at the quilting circle."

"Call me once you two talk."

Once they talked? Ben doubted there'd be much talking going on once he asked Chloe if she'd attempted suicide. No matter how he tried to couch the question, he was pretty sure it wouldn't be taken well.

They stepped into the reception hall, the buzz of activity and enthusiasm washing over Ben. He loved watching the women and men as they worked, the busy, almost frantic pace they set like an intricately choreographed dance to the music of chattering voices and laughter.

"There's my wife." Jake's soft smile and quick, eager steps as he moved toward Tiffany brought back memories of Ben's own happiness with Theresa, his own eagerness to be with her.

Now, he had no one to rush to. No one waiting for his return home. No one to ask about his day. He'd had seven years to get used to that, but sometimes it still bothered him. Sometimes he still felt the aching pain of loss and loneliness.

He shook aside the thoughts, not willing to dwell on what he didn't have. The key to happiness and contentment, he'd found, was in dwelling on what he *did* have. A home. Friends. A job he loved.

He scanned the room, searching for Chloe's coal-black hair and slim figure, not sure he'd be able to spot her in the crowd if she were there. A few men were interspersed among the women, mostly widowers, though some were young teenagers or college students. One or two die-hard bachelors were in the mix as well, looking for someone new to set their sights on. Ben searched their faces, wondering if Brian McMath were there. If he was, he'd probably hightail it to the only single woman in attendance who didn't know his reputation.

It took only a few seconds to spot the doctor, his buttoned-up white dress shirt and dark tie setting him apart from the rest of the crowd. Standing at the stuffing table, shoving filler into a quilted bear, Brian looked like a fish out of water. The woman beside him looked more comfortable, her faded jeans and dark sweater more in keeping with what the rest of the group was wearing.

Chloe.

Both surprised and pleased to see her there, Ben strode toward the two. "Hi Brian. Chloe. Mind if I join you?"

"Actually, we were discussing some medical issues that Chloe would probably prefer to keep private." McMath's dismissal was curt.

Ben ignored it.

"Sounds fascinating." He smiled at Chloe and she returned the gesture, her lips curving, her eyes begging for intervention.

"Not even close. Here," She handed him a flat bear patchworked in various yellow prints. "You can stuff Cheers. He's starting to feel left out."

"Cheers?"

"He's bright enough to cheer anyone up."

"Did you name yours, too?" He gestured toward the purple-toned bear she held.

"Of course. This one is Hugs."

"Because he'd make any kid want to hug him?"

"You catch on quick, Ben." This time her smile was real.

"I hate to break the news to you two, but they're stuffed bears. They don't require names."

Chloe met Ben's eyes and her smile widened. "Of course they do. That's the whole point of having a stuffed animal. You give it a name. Pretend it's your friend."

"Must be a girl thing." Brian grumbled and grabbed another handful of filler.

"I don't know about that. I can remember having a stuffed bear when I was maybe five. I called him Brown Bear." He'd given it to his sister when she was a toddler and she'd recently passed it to her one-year-old.

"Brown Bear. Very creative, Ben. My toys were more educational. Puzzles. Word games. Those kinds of things. How about you, Chloe? I'm sure a computer forensic expert…"

"I'm a florist, Brian."

"But you *were* an expert in computer forensics. I'm sure the kind of intelligence it takes to do that sort of work starts in early childhood."

"Actually, I didn't have many toys when I was a kid. Just a stuffed turtle that Opal gave me. A floppy green and brown one that was perfect for cuddling."

"And you named him, of course." Ben shoved a handful of stuffing into the yellow bear, wondering if the bright, relaxed woman next to him was really the tragically broken woman the D.C. police had painted her to be.

"Of course. I called him Speedy."

"That's a strange name for a turtle." Brian frowned, tossed the green bear he was stuffing onto the table where another group was stitching closed openings. "But let's talk about something that is more grown-up. Like those scars. There are ways to correct some of the damage, Chloe."

"I'm sure there are, but I'm not interested." Chloe finished stuffing the bear she was working on and grabbed the last one off the table, slashes of color staining her cheeks.

"Surely a woman as beautiful as you—"

"Knows her own mind." Ben spoke firmly, hoping to put an end to Brian's pushiness.

"Like I said when you joined us, the conversation is confidential. Something between patient and doctor."

"You're right, Brian. I think that's exactly what I'll do. Discuss things with my doctor." Chloe finished filling the last bear and set it on the to-be-stitched table, her smile sweet as pecan pie, but not quite hiding the bite to her words.

"I'm sure you haven't had time to find one yet."

"My surgeon recommended someone. I've got an appointment for next week."

"I see. Who with?"

"I think that's probably confidential, Brian." Ben smiled at the doctor, then gestured to the empty table. "It looks like we've finished the last bear. How about joining me for a cup of coffee, Chloe?"

Chloe's brow creased, a frown pulling at the edges of her mouth. Ben thought she'd refuse. Then she glanced at Brian and nodded. "Sure. It was nice talking to you, Brian."

"Maybe we'll see each other next week."

"Maybe."

"I'll see you Sunday, Brian."

The doctor's nod was curt, his shoulders stiff as he moved away.

"I guess we should go get that coffee." Chloe sounded tired, the dark shadows under her eyes speaking of too many sleepless nights.

"You don't seem too enthusiastic."

"It's been a long day."

"Opal's working you too hard?"

"You know that isn't even close to the truth."

"I do." He led her into the office, gestured for her to have a seat. "So maybe she's not working you hard enough."

"Boredom *can* make the day long, but I wasn't bored

today. We're almost too busy this week what with half of Lakeview coming in to hear about what happened Saturday night."

"So if it's not boredom maybe there were too many thorns on the roses. Too many petals in your hair."

She smiled, shook her head. "Too many nightmares last night."

"I'd like to say that was going to be my next guess, but it wasn't." He poured coffee from the carafe on the coffee-maker and handed her a cup. "Want to tell me about them?"

"Not really." She smiled again, lowering her gaze and tracing a circle on the desk with her finger. "You and Jake walked into the reception hall together."

"He stopped by to see his wife."

"He had news, though. About me, right?"

"He did say he'd spoken to D.C. police again."

"And?" She met his gaze, her eyes shadowed, whatever she was thinking well-hidden.

He could beat around the bush or he could lay it all out on the table. The latter was more his style and Ben couldn't think of a good reason to change it now. Much as he might want to avoid the issue, he wasn't going to hide the truth. "The guy he spoke to today said you tried to commit suicide."

"I knew that would come up eventually."

"Yet you didn't mention it to Jake."

"And give him reason to doubt me? I lived with that for almost eleven months. I didn't want to live it here, too." She brushed her bangs off her forehead, her eyes flashing emerald green fire.

"Like Jake told you before, he can't help you if he doesn't have all the necessary information."

"He knows everything I do."

"Everything except whether or not you actually were attempting suicide."

"If I'd been trying to kill myself, I wouldn't have picked up the phone and had a conversation with Opal." Her words were blunt, her gaze direct, but there was a forced quality to both, as if she were trying to convince herself of the very things she wanted him to believe.

"I believe you."

"Do you? Because lately I'm not even sure I believe myself." She stood abruptly. "I've really got to go. Like I said, it's been a long day."

Ben stood, too, putting a hand on Chloe's arm and holding her in place when she would have walked out the door. Her skin was pale, her mouth drawn in a tight line, the moisture in her eyes tempting Ben to wrap her in a hug that he knew she wouldn't appreciate. "Whatever is going on, Chloe, you don't have to face it alone."

"I appreciate the thought, but all the platitudes in the world can't change the fact that I *am* facing it alone."

"I don't believe in placating people. I believe in telling the truth."

"What truth? That you and Jake are going to help me? That God is looking out for me? I've trusted the police before. I've trusted God. But it hasn't done me any good. The nightmare is still chasing me. Eventually, it's going to catch up." There was no anger in her voice, just a weariness that Ben knew all too well. "I really do need to go."

He nodded, reluctantly letting his hand slide from her arm. "Your apartment is only five minutes from here. If anything happens and you need help fast, give me a call." He grabbed a sheet of paper from his desk and scribbled his home and cell phone number on it.

"Thanks."

"I'll be praying for you, Chloe."

"Thanks for that, too. I guess I'll see you Saturday?"

"I wouldn't miss it."

She nodded and stepped out of the office.

Ben pulled the door closed, wishing he could do more than offer words and friendship, wishing she would accept more. But he couldn't, she wouldn't, and he knew the best thing he could do for both of them was pray.

Lord, I don't know why my life has intersected with Chloe's. I don't know what Your purpose is for us, but I know there is one. I pray that Your will be done in both our lives and that in Your infinite mercy You will give Chloe the faith she needs to overcome whatever obstacles and challenges she faces.

The prayer was simple, the peace that washed over Ben a familiar friend. He took a seat behind his desk, tapping a pen against his palm, the glimmer of an idea forming. He smiled, grabbed the phone and dialed.

TEN

Chloe paced the length of her living room for the fifth time, the walls pressing in on her, the darkness beyond the window preventing her from doing what she wanted to do—leave.

Exhaustion dragged her down, but the bone-deep ache in her thigh wouldn't allow her to sink into sleep. The skin on her neck felt tight, the bands of scars uncomfortably stiff. She wanted to blame both on her work at Blooming Baskets, but being on her feet for a few hours a day wasn't the cause. Neither was bending over flower arrangements. Anxiety. Tension. Fear. They haunted her days and filled her nights with dreams that stayed in her mind long after she woke.

She moved toward the computer that sat on the desk against one wall of the living room. Maybe she should e-mail a few friends, catch up with them. Make a few phone calls. See how everyone was, but that would mean explaining all that had happened in the past month. Explaining that she'd left town because she hadn't attempted suicide. Explaining that someone wanted her dead.

The story sounded far-fetched even to her.

She grimaced, stalked into her bedroom and picked up her Bible before returning to the living room and pushing open the balcony door. The full moon cast bluish light across the yard and reflected off the lake, painting the world in shades of gray. If she'd had her camera, she would have taken a picture, but she didn't and instead she tried to soak it all in, memorize it, pack it away in her mind so that she could take it with her if she was forced to run again.

The phone rang, the sound drifting out onto the balcony and offering a welcome distraction.

She hurried to pick it up. "Hello?"

"Chloe? It's Ben." The warmth of his voice washed over her, and she sank down into the recliner, relaxing for the first time in what seemed like hours.

"Hi. What's up?"

"I was just out for a ride and thought I'd give you a call."

"Opal must have put you up to it."

"No, but she did give me your number."

"I bet you didn't have to twist her arm for it."

"Not even a little."

Chloe smiled, enjoying the conversation more than she knew was good for her. "So, if Opal didn't put you up to calling me, who did?"

"Me. I had a thought after you left the church the other night and I wanted to share it with you."

"I'm all ears."

"It'll be hard to explain over the phone. What would you say to going for a ride with me?"

"Now?"

"You're not busy. I'm not busy. What better time than now?"

Chloe glanced toward the still-open balcony door and the darkness beyond. "I don't usually go out at night. The darkness hides too much."

She spoke without thinking, her cheeks heating as she realized what she'd said. "What I meant was—"

"No need to explain. Let's do it another time."

"You haven't even said what *it* is."

"And ruin the surprise?"

"I'm not much for surprises." Most of the ones she'd had weren't good.

He chuckled, the warmth of it seeping through the phone line and tugging at Chloe's heart. "I had a feeling you were going to tell me you didn't like surprises. So, here's the thing, I have a friend who's a veterinarian. She's got a litter of puppies she needs to find homes for."

"Puppies?"

"Puppies. As in little yapping bundles of fur."

"Should I ask what this has to do with me?"

"I thought you might like some company at night. A puppy seemed perfect."

"I've never had a dog. I wouldn't know the first thing about taking care of one." Though she had to admit, the idea held a certain appeal. The past few nights had been long, filled with odd noises and sinister shadows, nightmares and memories. A distraction might be just what she needed.

"There's a first time for everything, Chloe." There was a smile in Ben's voice and Chloe's lips curved in response.

"My landlady might not allow pets."

"The Andersons across the hall from you have one. They've brought it to a couple of church picnics."

"The little mop they dress in a sweater doesn't qualify as a pet."

His laughter rumbled out again. "Tell you what, why don't you think about it? You can give me a call, or we can talk about it when we get together for dinner."

She should definitely think about it. Rushing into something like a puppy could only lead to trouble and regret, and she had enough of both of those to last a lifetime.

She didn't *want* to think about it, though, because saying no would mean spending another night alone in the apartment. Another night jumping at every sound, wondering about every shadow. "Is the offer still open for tonight?"

"Sure."

"Then I think I'll take you up on it."

"Great. I'll be there in five."

Five minutes was just enough time for Chloe to check her copy of the rental agreement she'd signed, pull on shoes, pop two aspirin and waffle back and forth on the puppy idea a dozen times.

By the time Ben knocked, she'd driven herself crazy with indecision. Over a dog. But she couldn't deny the excitement she felt. The sense of fun and adventure that had been missing from her life for far too long and now welled up inside as she pulled the door open. "Five minutes on the dot."

"I'm a stickler for being on time. Ready?" His easy smile was as familiar as an old friend's and just as welcome.

"Indecisive." She limped over and grabbed her purse off the couch, pulled on a jacket.

"Then it's good you don't have to decide anything tonight." Despite his smile, Ben seemed more subdued than usual, his normally abundant charm overshadowed by something dark and sad.

"Is everything okay?"

"Yes." But it wasn't. Fatigue had darkened his eyes from sapphire to navy. Tension bracketed his mouth. "We'd better get going. Tori said she'd be at the clinic until eight-thirty. I don't want to keep her longer than that."

Chloe nodded, stepping out into the hallway and moving down the steps toward the front door, knowing she shouldn't ask the questions that were clamoring through her mind, but unable to stop herself. "Were you working today?"

"Friday's the day I do visitations. We've got several housebound members of the congregation and a few in the hospital." He paused, ran a hand over his hair. "I also conducted a funeral for a two-year-old boy."

"Just a baby. That's terrible."

He nodded, his jaw tight. "It's hard enough to say goodbye to someone who has lived a long, full life. Saying goodbye to a child who has barely begun to live is devastating."

"I can't even imagine what that must be like for the parents."

"Me, neither." He pushed open the front door, his movements stiff. "Talking to people who are so devastated, so desperate to know why the tragedy happened, how God could have allowed it, is tough, because there are no answers. We live in a fallen sinful world. Tragedy is part of that. We know that God loves us, that He wants what's best for us. That makes accepting things like a child's death even more difficult."

He ran a hand over his face, then stepped out onto the porch. "Maybe tonight isn't such a good night for this, after all. I came to cheer you up, not drag you down into the pit with me."

Chloe hesitated, then put her hand on his arm, feeling the rigid tension of the muscles beneath his sleeve. "I was already in the pit before you arrived. Since we're both in it together, we may as well hang out. Who knows? Maybe we'll manage to hoist each other out."

Ben stared down at her, his eyes dark, the angles of his face harsher in the porch light. He looked harder, tougher, much more like the teen he'd said he'd been than the man he'd become.

Finally, he shrugged. "Then let's go look at puppies."

He started down the porch steps and Chloe followed, the coolness of the evening seeping through the long-sleeved blouse and lightweight jacket she wore. She shivered, stumbling down the first step, her bad leg buckling.

Ben grabbed her arm before she could fall the rest of the way. "Whoa! Careful. If you fall and break your leg, Opal will have my hide."

"And my surgeon will have *mine*." She limped down the last two steps, pausing at the bottom to let the aching pain in her thigh ease. "She spent a lot of hours putting it back together. She won't be happy if I undo all that work."

"Then we definitely need to make sure it doesn't get broken again."

"I don't think we have to worry about it too much. I've got enough rods and screws in it to set off a metal detector."

"Sounds pretty indestructible, but let's not take any chances." He put a hand under her elbow and led her to his sedan, his slow pace matching her limping stride.

Even with Ben beside her, Chloe felt fear creeping close, breathing a dire warning in her ear. Something was out here with them. Something dark and evil. Something ready to strike. Ready to kill.

She glanced around the yard, searching for signs of danger. There was nothing there. At least nothing she could see.

As if he sensed it, too, Ben stilled, his body tense. "Something seems off."

"Off?"

"Yeah. Off. And it's crawling up my spine and shouting a warning in my ear." He glanced around the yard, the hardness Chloe had seen while he stood on the porch even more pronounced.

"Come on." He hurried her toward the car, pulled open the door. "Get in."

Chloe did as he asked, sliding into the sedan and expecting him to do the same.

"Lock the door. I want to take a look around." He pushed the door closed, but Chloe caught it before it could snap shut, pushing it open once again.

"Look around? For what?"

"For whatever it is that's out here with us."

"Ben, I don't think that's a good idea. Let's go inside and call the police."

"Use my cell phone to call. It's in the glove compartment. I've got Jake's number on speed dial. Lock the door and stay in the car until I get back."

"Let's call him together. You can't go running after whoever is out there by yourself."

"Why not? It won't be the first time I've gone running after something lurking in the darkness."

"I didn't realize that was part of a pastor's job description." Chloe wanted to grab Ben's hand and keep him from leaving.

"It isn't. Good thing I haven't always been a pastor." He brushed the bangs from her eyes and smiled, his teeth flashing white in the darkness. "Now, stop worrying and stay put."

With that he shut the door and started across the yard toward the lake.

Chloe watched him go, sure that at any moment someone would swoop down on him. Instead, he seemed to disappear, blending into the shadows and fading into the night. Chloe found the cell phone, scrolling through the contact numbers until she found Jake's.

He picked up quickly, his gruff voice filling her with relief. "Reed here."

"It's Chloe. Davidson."

"Calling from Ben's cell phone. Is he okay?"

"I don't know," she explained quickly, her words rushing out so that she wasn't sure Jake would be able to make any sense of them.

"You're at your place?"

"Yes."

"Stay where you are. I'll be there in ten."

Ten minutes. Six hundred seconds. Plenty of time for a shot to be fired, a knife to be buried deep in a chest. A man to die.

Images filled Chloe's head. Black night. Fire. A shadowy figure. Danger. Pain.

Fear.

She wanted to sink down in the seat, hide her head until help arrived. Wanted to embrace the weak-willed, wimpy woman she'd become and let Ben and Jake handle the problem.

Wanted to, but couldn't.

Adam had died because of her investigation into the death of Ana Benedict, had died because of what that investigation had uncovered about The Strangers. She had no intention of letting the same thing happen to Ben. Fear or no fear, she was getting out of the car and she was going to face whatever was hiding in the darkness.

Hands shaking, she shoved open the car door and took a gulping breath of cool air. The yard was silent and still, waiting for whatever would come. Chloe waited, too, breathless and watching, hoping to see Ben return before she actually had to go after him. Finally, she couldn't put it off any longer and she stepped away from the car, leaves and grass crunching under her feet, releasing the heavy scent of earth and decay.

Up ahead, the dark water of the lake washed over rocks and wood, lapping against the shore in rhythmic waves that should have been soothing but weren't.

I could really use some help right about now, Lord.

The prayer chanted through her mind as she skirted a thick grove of trees and approached the lake. The shoreline was empty, tall reeds and thick grasses heavy and overgrown, tangled in bunches near the water's edge. A boat bobbed on the surface of the lake, the rickety dock it was tied to barely keeping it from floating away.

"Ben?" She whispered his name as she moved toward the dock, peering into the shadows afraid of what she might find there.

"I thought you were staying in the car."

He spoke from behind her, his voice so unexpected, Chloe bit back a scream, whirling to face him, her heart in her throat. "I didn't want you to be out here by yourself."

"So you decided to come out by *yourself?*" The moon was behind him, casting shadows across his face, making his expression impossible to read.

"It seemed like a good idea at the time."

"It wasn't." He cupped her elbow, tugging her back toward the house.

"Did you see someone?"

"No, but that doesn't mean someone wasn't here."

"What do we do now?"

"We go back to the car and you get in it and lock the door. I walk around the house and see if there's any evidence that someone has been hanging around. Maybe talk to the downstairs tenant, see if he's heard anything. Once Jake gets here and checks things out, we'll head over the veterinary clinic."

"It's getting a little late for that."

"It's not late at all." His hand rested on her back, the warmth of it seeping through her jacket and warming her chilled skin. "I hear sirens. Jake is on the way. Stay in the car this time, okay?"

"Okay."

The door shut again and this time Chloe stayed where she was, watching Ben move around the perimeter of the house as the sound of sirens drifted into the car and her rapidly beating heart subsided.

ELEVEN

By the time Jake and Ben finished searching the property, Chloe had come up with several excuses to return to her apartment and lock herself in for the night. Her head ached. Her leg throbbed. She really didn't think a puppy was a good idea.

All of them fled her mind as Ben pulled open the car door and slid in, a woodsy, masculine scent floating into the car with him. "We're all set."

"Did you find anything?"

"Nothing but a few smudged footprints near the window under your apartment. They could be from anyone and could have been there for a few days." He started the engine. "Someone was out there tonight, though. I'm sure of it."

"You saw someone?"

"Felt someone. Whether or not that someone has anything to do with what's been happening to you, I can't say."

"How could it not? It's exactly what's been happening to me for months."

"It started after the accident?"

Had it? It seemed that what had happened after the accident was crystal clear, the threat she felt like a waking nightmare she couldn't escape from. What had come before was less clear and Chloe couldn't say for sure that she hadn't felt the same way. She couldn't say she had, either. "I don't know."

"The man who was convicted of murder—"

"Matthew Jackson." His pale face and coal-black eyes were tattooed into her memory, his skeletal frame standing outside the burning car, something she would never forget.

"According to the news reports I heard, Jackson never admitted to sabotaging your car. It's possible he didn't."

"He was there, Ben. Standing outside the car while it burned around us. He had a gun." The police speculated that he'd been planning to kill Chloe if she got out of the car. The fire that had scarred her, had saved her life. The bent metal that had held her inside the burning wreck had kept her from certain death.

The thought made her shudder and she wrapped her arms around her waist. "Jackson wanted me dead. He was at the scene of the accident. It seems pretty obvious he had something to do with it."

"Maybe he did, but maybe the accident has nothing to do with what's happening now." Ben turned into the parking lot of a well-lit building and turned to face her. "What if the D.C. police were heading in the wrong direction? What if they couldn't find evidence that you were being stalked because they were looking for a connection to Jackson and couldn't find it?"

She rubbed the ache in her thigh, wincing a little as bunched muscles contracted even more. "They looked in every direction. My old caseload, my personal relationships. They investigated thoroughly but couldn't find anyone else who had a grudge against me."

"Did you?"

"Did I what?"

"Investigate." His eyes were liquid fire in the dim light, his face carved from stone, but his hand was gentle as it wrapped around hers, his fingers skimming across her palm and settling there. "It's what you do. It would seem natural for you to check things out yourself."

"I was too sick at first. By the time I was healthy enough to think about investigating, Jackson was in jail and it seemed the police had covered all the bases."

"If it were my life on the line, I don't think I'd rely solely on the police to investigate." His hand dropped away from hers and he opened his door. "This is it. Tori's clinic. Let's head in and see what those puppies are like."

Chloe grabbed his arm before he could get out, scowling as he turned to face her. "You're good, Ben Avery. Really good. But I know exactly what you're up to and…" She planned on saying it wasn't going to work, that she had no intention of digging into her old caseloads, no intention of searching for someone who might want her dead. But he'd planted a seed and it was already growing in the fallow soil of her heart.

"And what?" His gaze touched her hair, her cheeks, her lips, lingering there for a second before he met her eyes.

Her skin heated, but she ignored it and the wild beating of her heart. "And it's working. But I use computer forensics to investigate crime. If someone is really coming after me, that won't be hidden in a computer file or found in a deleted e-mail."

"But his reason might be."

He had a good point and Chloe mulled it over as she got out of the car. "I'll have to look through my open cases. Maybe I'll find something there."

"If you do, go to Jake with it. Don't try to confront the person yourself."

"I'm not *that* crazy. One near-death experience in a lifetime is more than enough."

He chuckled and pressed a hand to Chloe's lower spine. "Come on. Tori is probably pacing the floor wondering what's taking so long."

"Maybe she's left." Which might be a good thing.

"Maybe, but it's doubtful. She's got to find homes for these puppies before her grandfather finds another litter."

"Her grandfather brought her the puppies?"

"Yeah. That was this week. Last week, he found an abandoned potbellied pig. The week before he found a goat."

"What's he do? Ride around looking for strays?"

"When he's not riding around looking for Opal."

"Opal?"

"Yeah. Sam's got a thing for her. You probably remember meeting him the night of the wedding. Tall, gray hair, smitten look on his face."

"I remember. I tried to find out what's going on with them, but Opal is keeping mum."

"That's probably for the best."

"Why's that?"

"It'll give you an excuse to keep mum about what's going on with us." He shouldered open the clinic door, gesturing for Chloe to precede him into the brightly lit reception area.

"Nothing is going on with us."

"I'm not so sure you're right about that, Chloe." He smiled, the gentle curve of his lips spearing into Chloe's heart.

She blinked, took a step back, denying what she was feeling. Refusing it. She didn't need to add a man to her already complicated life. She *wouldn't* add a man to it. "Ben—"

"You're finally here. I was beginning to wonder if you were coming at all." A woman strode toward them, her movements brisk despite what looked like an advanced pregnancy. Tall and striking with bright red hair and green eyes, she exuded confidence and warmth as she offered a hand to Chloe. "You must be Chloe. I'm Tori Stone. You met my grandfather the other night."

"I remember."

"Yeah, well, Sam is hard to forget. The puppies are this way. I've only got two left. This litter has been pretty easy to place. The last one…" She paused, shuddered. "Not so much."

"Was something wrong with them?"

"Wrong? No. They were just homely. Poor little guys. Eventually we found some people who were willing to overlook that." She smiled, led them to a closed door. "Here we are. I've got a few patients to check on. I'll let you two take a look. Then come back in a few minutes to see what you think."

She pushed open the door and motioned for Chloe to go in. "Feel free to take them out of the crate, but close the door if you do or they'll be down the hall and into trouble before you know it. See you in a few."

Chloe stepped into the room. It housed an exam table, cabinets, a counter. The crate sat on the floor near the far wall, the wiggling, squirming balls of fur inside it looking more like overgrown dust bunnies than dogs.

"Those are puppies? They look more like miniature mops or giant dust bunnies to me." Ben's comment neatly mimicked what Chloe was thinking, and she smiled.

"Except for the tails."

"There is that." Ben knelt down. "Which do you want to see? The fuzzy one or the fuzzier one."

"Either."

Ben reached in and pulled out a handful of wiggling cream-colored puppy. "Try this one."

She lifted it to her chest, stroking silky fur and feeling the vibrating excitement of the puppy surge through her. It strained against her hold, licking her hands and neck and rolling sideways for a belly rub. "It's awfully cute."

"So's this one." Ben lifted out the second pup and set it on the floor. Its paws were black, its torso dark brown, its tail wagging so fast, Chloe thought it might knock itself over.

"If I *were* to decide to bring one home I wouldn't know which to choose." Chloe set the one she was holding down, and watched as it scampered across the floor, rushing from wall to wall, skidding on the tile floor and slamming into the door.

Chloe laughed, kneeling down, her bad leg protesting the move. She ignored it, picking up the brown puppy and holding it up so she could look in its eyes. "This one is quieter."

"Definitely."

She put it back down, smiling as it climbed up her legs and settled down for a nap. "I don't know, Ben. They're both adorable, but I'm not sure I'm ready for a pet."

"Ever have one before?"

"Not even a fish. The closest I came to it was Speedy."

"The stuffed turtle."

"Exactly."

Ben lifted the cream-colored puppy and rubbed it under

its chin as he settled down beside Chloe. "Like I said before, there's a first time for everything."

"I'm just not sure now is the right time for this particular first."

"It's your decision to make." He placed the puppy down on the floor, watching as it raced away. "But it might be fun to have a quirky little guy like that racing around the apartment."

A soft knock sounded on the door and Tori strode in. "I see you've met Cain and Abel."

She knelt down next to Chloe, smoothing the fur on the dark puppy's back. "They're brothers, but the similarity ends there. Cain is full of energy and life. Lovable but constantly in trouble."

"Then this one must be Abel." Chloe stroked the puppy's head.

"Yes. Sweet as pie. Cute as a button. Smart as a whip." She grinned. "But lazy."

"They're both sweet as pie."

"You're right about that, Chloe, but their personalities are very different. If you decide you want to take one, you need to think about which will fit better with your lifestyle."

Chloe nodded, watching Cain as he chased his tail. His energy level high, his exuberance appealing. A year or two ago, he would have been her choice. Now, though, she wasn't sure she could keep up with the wiggling ball of energy. The quieter puppy, on the other hand, was more her speed, his slow movements as he finally roused himself to join his brother's play made her smile.

"You don't have to make up your mind tonight, of course. I can hold them both for a few days while you decide." Tori started to rise and Ben hurried to offer a hand up. "Thanks, Ben. Why don't I give you a couple more minutes with the puppies? Then we'll call it a night."

The door closed behind Tori's retreating figure.

"What do you think?" Ben lifted Cain and rubbed his belly.

"I think you should take that one home with you."

"We didn't come here to pick a puppy for me. We came for you. You need some company, remember?"

"And you don't?"

"My life is busy. I don't have time for a puppy."

"Mine is, too, and neither do I."

"So, I guess we leave them here."

"I guess we do." She lifted the brown puppy who'd come to sit in her lap again, surprised by the disappointment she felt. "Sorry, guy."

"Of course, there's another option." Ben knelt down in front of Chloe, lifting Abel from her arms and setting him on the floor.

"What's that?"

"We could *make* time for them." He grabbed Chloe's hand and tugged her to her feet, his hands wrapping around her waist to hold her steady.

"Come on, Chloe. You know you want to." His grin was just the right side of wicked, his eyes flashing with amusement and a challenge Chloe knew she should ignore, but couldn't.

"So you're saying if I take Abel, you'll take Cain?"

"I'm saying if you take one I'll take the other. Which one of us gets the hyperactive guy is up for debate."

"Debate? I think it's pretty obvious that the more active puppy should go to the more able-bodied person. My bum leg won't let me chase after anything much faster than Abel."

"You may have a point. One way or another, we'll have to work out visitation. A couple of walks a week. Maybe a playdate or two." He leaned a shoulder against the wall. "Just because you and I aren't together, doesn't mean the boys shouldn't be able to spend time with each other."

He looked serious, his face set in somber lines, sandy hair falling over his forehead, but laughter danced in his eyes.

Chloe's own laughter bubbled out, spilling into the room, the feeling of it new and fresh. Life, hope, joy. So many things she'd thought she'd never have again, but that suddenly seemed possible. Here, in the brightly lit room, two puppies scampering near her feet, Ben's amused eyes staring into hers, she could almost forget the darkness that waited outside, the shadows that seemed determined to follow her wherever she went.

Almost.

"Don't stop." He brushed strands of hair from Chloe's cheeks, his fingers lingering for a moment before dropping away.

"Stop what?"

"Laughing. It's good for the soul."

"I guess I need to find more things to laugh about, then."

"You will. Sorrow fades in time."

"Sorrow I can handle. It's the guilt that's eating me alive."

"You've got nothing to feel guilty about."

"Don't I?" She leaned down and scooped Abel into her arms, the fuzzy warmth of the puppy comforting. "My investigation caused Adam's death."

"The person who sabotaged your car caused his death."

"No matter which way you try to paint the picture, it'll always be the same. I found information that I passed on to the FBI. Because of that The Strangers dismantled.

Because of *that*, Matthew Jackson tried to kill me and killed Adam instead."

"It seems to me you're taking a lot of responsibility for something you couldn't know would happen."

"I'm not taking responsibility. I'm just…"

"What?"

"Wishing I'd made different choices. Wishing that Adam hadn't died in my place."

Ben's hands framed her face, the rough calluses on his palms rasping against her skin. "He didn't die in your place, Chloe. He was killed in a tragic accident that had nothing to do with you and everything to do with someone else's sin."

"The words sound good, Ben, but they don't feel like the truth."

"Then it's good that how we feel doesn't actually determine the facts." His hands slid to her neck, his thumbs brushing against the tender flesh under her jaw and spreading warmth in their wake.

Chloe's heart jumped, and she stepped back, refusing to put a name to what she'd promised herself she'd never feel again. "We should find Tori and tell her we've decided to take the puppies."

For a moment, she didn't think Ben was going to acknowledge her comment. His vivid eyes stared into hers, secrets and shadows hidden in their depth.

Finally, he nodded. "Let me corral Cain first."

Chloe waited at the door, Abel sleeping in her arms, his fuzzy head pressed into the crook of her elbow, her heartbeat slowing, the places where Ben's hands had rested cooling. She shouldn't be letting him affect her so much, shouldn't be having this kind of reaction to him.

Shouldn't be, but it didn't seem she had much of a choice. No matter how much she might want to tell herself differently, Ben was becoming a fixture in her life. She wasn't sure she liked it and was even less sure she could change it. All she *could* do was pray that Ben wouldn't eventually suffer for being her friend and that she wouldn't eventually be left heartbroken again.

TWELVE

Having a puppy in the apartment proved to be as much of a distraction as Ben had said it would be. The cozy rooms Chloe loved so much were even more inviting with a ball of fur keeping her company in them.

And company was definitely something she needed at three in the morning when nightmares woke her and fear kept her from returning to sleep.

She shifted in the easy chair, hoping a change in position would alleviate the ache in her leg. Abel whined, moving into a more comfortable spot, his body heat seeping through the flannel pajamas Chloe wore and easing the knotted muscles of her thigh.

"You're a living heating pad, puppy." His tail thumped, his eyes opened briefly before he went back to sleep again.

Chloe wished she could do the same, but the dream she'd woken from refused to release its hold and her heart hammered in response, the quick, sickening thud enough to convince her she was having a heart attack. She wasn't. Despite the pressure in her chest, the too-rapid throb of her pulse and the cold sweat that beaded her brow, she knew she was suffering from nothing more than panic.

She wanted to get up and move, pace the floor, run a

mile, talk to someone. She lifted the phone, realized what she was doing and set it down again. She couldn't call Opal at this time of the morning. Not when Opal was already so worried about Chloe's mental health. She wouldn't call Ben. All she could do was sit and wait while seconds became minutes and minutes hours.

Or she could use the time to do what Ben had suggested. She could pull her laptop from the closet where she'd shoved it when she'd moved in and revisit the cases she'd been working on around the time of the accident. As much as she wanted to believe that Matthew Jackson had been convicted of a crime he *had* committed, Ben had planted a seed of doubt and Chloe couldn't ignore it no matter how much she wanted to.

And the fact was, she really didn't want to.

It was a surprising change to the head-in-the-sand attitude she'd taken for so long; Chloe's mood lifted as a small spark of the person she'd once been took hold, urging her to face the situation, sort out the facts and find out for herself what was what, who was who and just how she could keep herself alive.

Maybe coming to Lakeview had given her back some of her old confidence and enthusiasm. Maybe talking to Ben had. Or maybe as her physical health and strength returned, her will to survive was kicking in stronger than ever. Whatever the case, Chloe was an investigator. She'd spent almost a decade of her life seeking evidence and answers. She'd found them for the FBI, for private investigators, for the police. Now she was going to find them for herself.

"Sorry, pup, you're going to have to move." She stood, setting Abel down on the ground and moving to her bedroom. The puppy scampered after her, waddling into the closet when she opened the door, pawing at the box she pulled out.

"This is mine, Abel. Tomorrow we'll get you some fun toys to play with."

Abel tilted his head to one side as if he were actually listening, Chloe smiled. "It's good to know I won't be talking to myself anymore. Come on. We've got work to do."

She grabbed her laptop from the box and carried it to the kitchen. Her hands were shaking as she set it up on the tiny table there. It wasn't fear that made them tremble. Excitement, anticipation, the drive to succeed— all the things that had made her good at computer forensics—those were what had her hands shaking and her heart racing.

Her elbow hit the Bible she'd set on the edge of the table and she shoved it away, then paused, pulling it back toward her, the yearning she'd felt since she'd come to Lakeview as real and as tangible as anything she might find stored on the computer.

After Adam's betrayal, she'd prayed for understanding, prayed that she could accept what had happened and move on. In those dark moments, she'd felt sure that God was listening, that He understood and cried with her. Then Adam had been killed and that certainty had been ripped away, a gaping hole all that remained of her fragile faith.

But maybe faith couldn't disappear or fade away. Maybe it couldn't be ripped from a life. Maybe, like the information she pulled from computer systems, it was only hidden from sight, waiting for a little effort, a little attention, to bring it back into view again.

She pushed the laptop toward the center of the table, opened her Bible to the first chapter of John and started reading.

"You've caught the biggest fish again, friend." Ben eyed Jake's cooler full of fish and his own empty one.

"Again? If I remember correctly, you've brought in the biggest catch three times running."

"You may be right, but that doesn't make my loss this time any less painful." He stepped out onto the dock, tied the boat. "I guess I'll be heading to the grocery store before I cook dinner for Chloe. Preparing store-bought fish after a fishing trip isn't a very manly thing to do, but I'll swallow my pride and do it."

"Your pitiful act is falling on deaf ears."

"Anyone ever tell you you're coldhearted?"

"Not coldhearted. Practical. The way I see it, if you want a couple of my fish, you'll have to trade for them."

"A trade or a trip to the grocery store? I don't even need time to think about it. What do you want?"

"A babysitter. Tiffany's birthday is next week and I want to take her out. Unfortunately, her parents are going out of town and she doesn't trust just anyone to watch the kids."

"And you think she'll let me do it?"

"I *know* she will. I asked."

"You've got to be pretty desperate to be asking me, Jake. You do know I haven't changed a diaper in years? I'll probably end up putting it on backward or upside down."

"Desperation has nothing to do with it. You're the closest thing to a brother I've ever had. I trust you. Besides, Isaac is four weeks old. He won't care what way his diaper goes on."

"Since you put it that way, I guess I'll do it. No fish necessary."

"Thanks." Jake slapped him on the back and handed over the cooler filled with fish. "And just so we're clear, I would have given you these anyway."

"You say that *after* I've already committed to hours of diaper duty and baby-doll play." Which he had to admit he'd probably enjoy. *If* Isaac and his sister, Honor, didn't spend the entire time crying for their parents.

"Amazing how that worked out, isn't it?" Jake grinned and started toward his car. "Is six-thirty Friday okay with you?"

"I'll be there."

"Great. And now we'd both better get moving. I don't want to miss Honor's bath and I'm sure you don't want to be late for your date."

"Whoa! Hold up there. I'm cooking dinner for Chloe. That's not the same as a date."

"Then what *is* it the same as?"

"Cooking dinner for you and Tiffany or for my sister and Shane."

"Really? Because the way I see it, when you cook dinner for me and Tiffany or Raven and Shane, you're cooking for family. Chloe isn't family. So you cooking dinner for her doesn't seem like the same thing at all."

"She needs a friend. I'm being one."

"You just keep telling yourself that." Jake grinned and got into his car, his face sobering as he ran hand over his hair. "I hate to even ask, but did you ask Chloe about the suicide attempt?"

"She denied it."

"Do you believe her?"

"Yeah, I do."

"Then so do I. Which means we're dealing with a second murder attempt. We just have to find a way to prove it."

"Did the police in D.C. collect evidence?"

"It seemed like a cut-and-dry suicide attempt. They weren't looking for evidence of murder. When they went back in afterward, the place had been cleaned by some friends who were getting it ready for her return from the hospital."

"Convenient for the murderer. Do we know who those friends were?"

"You'll have to ask Chloe when you're there tonight. Or I'll give her a ring tomorrow."

"I'll ask."

"And I'll keep searching for answers. If Chloe's in danger, I plan to figure out where it's coming from.

"That makes two of us."

"You just be careful, friend. I'm a cop. You're not."

"I can handle myself." He might have left the military years ago, but he hadn't forgotten what he learned there.

Jake nodded, but the concern in his eyes didn't fade. "There's something going on here I don't like. Chloe's brought trouble into town. Big trouble. The fact that you're involved with her—"

"I'm not *involved* with anyone."

"You're cooking her dinner. You went and picked out puppies with her. You're involved, Ben, and that makes things all the more complicated." He scowled. "Like I said, be careful."

The car door shut before Ben could respond. That was probably for the best. There wasn't much left to say. Denying that he was involved with Chloe wouldn't convince Jake. The truth was, Ben wasn't all that convinced, either. Much as he might tell himself he wasn't interested in Chloe beyond wanting to help her adjust to her life in Lakeview, the truth seemed much more complex.

He was intrigued, compelled, drawn into the sadness he saw in her eyes, the laughter that must have come much more frequently before the tragedy.

Despite what she'd been through, she was strong, determined and dedicated to creating a better life for herself. Ben understood that. He'd lived it. Even her struggles with faith and trust were familiar to him. He understood Chloe and that wasn't something he could say about many of the women he'd met.

Whether or not that meant anything, whether or not he *wanted* it to mean anything remained to be seen. For right now, he'd enjoy spending a few hours with an interesting woman and not worry about what would come next. God had everything under control.

Ben just wasn't sure *he* did.

He sighed, hefted the cooler containing the fish and strode toward his car. Like Jake, he had a bad feeling about Chloe's situation. Her story was like a puzzle with missing pieces. Until the last one was found the picture would remain unclear. And until it *was* clear Ben wouldn't rest easy. Danger lurked around Chloe. He felt it every time he was near her. He couldn't see it and didn't know what direction it was coming from, but he knew it was there and that if they weren't careful it would destroy Chloe and anyone who stood in the way.

Fortunately, Ben planned to be careful. Really careful. He might not know what role Chloe was going to play in his life, but he knew exactly what role he planned to play in hers. He was going to keep her safe. A little caution and a lot of prayer would go a long way toward that. Dinner and puppy choosing were extra.

Speaking of which, he had some trout to cook and a dog to walk.

And a very attractive woman to spend the evening with. Despite his concerns, Ben couldn't help smiling as he got in his car and headed home.

THIRTEEN

Abel's soft whine commanded Chloe's attention and she glanced up from the file she was searching through. The puppy sat by the door, his head cocked to one side, his ears perked.

"You want to go out?"

Abel barked and scratched a paw against the door, his pint-size body vibrating with excitement.

"Sorry, buddy, you're going to have to wait. I took you out a half-hour ago and I don't plan to do the stairs again for a while."

Abel barked again. Chloe ignored him, choosing instead to stand and stretch tight, tense muscles. Her leg throbbed, her neck ached and she was sure she'd soon regret so many hours spent in one position, but right now all she felt was relief. She'd managed to search through sixteen files. All of them were cases that she'd been working on before the accident. Of those, four had caught and held her attention. Two were high-profile divorces, one involved tracing laundered funds and the last had required searching for evidence against a teacher who'd been accused of having a relationship with one of his students. In each case, Chloe'd been asked to retrieve information from the suspects' computers. Deleted e-mails, deleted files, things that most people assumed were gone could often still be found if one knew how to look. And Chloe definitely knew how to look.

She downed some cold coffee and limped back to her seat. Of the sixteen cases she'd been investigating, the ones that intrigued her were those she'd done the least amount of work on before the accident. Each of the four suspects had a lot to lose. A politician, a doctor, a respected business owner, a teacher with a wife and children. Any of them might have been desperate to keep his secrets hidden, but had one been desperate enough to commit murder? And if he had, what would cause him to keep coming after Chloe even after she'd dropped her investigation?

She didn't have answers to the questions, but at least she finally had questions. Until now, she'd been sliding closer and closer to believing she really was going crazy. Hopefully asking questions and seeking answers was the beginning of healing.

Abel barked again, jumping up against the door in what seemed like a desperate bid for escape.

"Am I that bad of company?"

A soft tap sounded on the wood and Abel tumbled backward, barking furiously and running for cover behind Chloe's legs.

"Some watchdog you are." Chloe scooped him up and strode toward the door. "Who's there?"

"Ben."

Ben? He wasn't supposed to be over until six. She glanced at the clock, realized that it *was* six and pulled open the door.

He looked as good as he had the night before, his sandy hair curling near his collar, his eyes blazing against his deeply tanned face. When he smiled, Chloe's heart melted into a puddle of yearning that she absolutely refused to acknowledge.

"Hi."

"Hi, yourself." He stepped into the living room, a cooler and brown paper bag in his arms, Cain nipping at the leash and tumbling along behind.

Ben glanced around the room, his gaze settling on the coffee table and the computer that sat there. Chloe had a notebook and pen lying next to it. A few crumbled sheets of paper were scattered on the table. One or two had dropped onto the floor. "Looks like you were working. Want to reschedule for another time?"

It would probably be for the best. Send Ben and his puppy on their way. Spend a few more hours doing research. Heat up a frozen meal and spend the rest of the evening alone. Those were safe and reasonable things to do. Unfortunately, Chloe didn't feel like being safe or reasonable. She felt like enjoying a couple of hours in the company of a man who demanded nothing more from her than conversation. "And miss out on a home-cooked meal? I don't think so."

"You don't usually do home cooked?"

"Only if heating things up in the microwave counts as home cooking."

Ben shook his head and smiled. "Not quite."

"I didn't think so. Opal says I'm culinary challenged. The fact is, I'm lazy. It seems like too much effort to cook a fancy meal for one."

"I'm with you on that. Cooking is much more fun when you're doing it for someone other than yourself." He stepped toward the kitchen, his tall, broad frame filling the room and stealing Chloe's breath.

She didn't understand it, didn't like it and was absolutely sure it could only mean trouble, but there was definitely something about Ben that drew her to him. His steadiness, his confidence, his faith, they were like blazing lights in what had become an ever-darkening world. When he was around, Chloe's anxiety and fear seemed to melt away; when he spoke, she could almost believe that everything was going to be okay.

It had been a long time since Chloe had felt that way around someone. Even before the accident she'd been self-reliant, depending on herself for the stability she craved. As much as she'd loved Adam, being with him had been more exciting than comforting, more stormy ocean than placid lake. They'd brought out the best in each other only when they weren't bringing out each others' worst. After he'd confessed to seeing another woman, Chloe finally acknowledged what she'd known all along—marrying him would send her right back into the chaotic life she'd worked so hard to escape.

"Are you okay?" Ben had moved back across the room and was standing in front of her, solid and warm. More real than nightmares or memories. More steady than Chloe's own rioting emotions.

"Fine. Just…" Confused? Scared? Guilty? All fit, but she wouldn't give them voice. "Sluggish. Sitting in front of the computer for too long does that to me."

He didn't believe her and she was sure he'd ask more questions, push for answers she wasn't sure she could give. Instead, he brushed her hair back from her face, hooking it behind her ears, his hands lingering on her shoulders, his thumbs resting against her collarbone. "I guess we'll have to do something about that."

To Chloe's horror an image flashed through her mind. Ben leaning close, his breath warm against her lips just before…

She shoved the thought away, her pulse accelerating, her cheeks heating as she stepped back. "What did you have in mind?"

"Nothing so horrible. Just a walk by the lake. I think the boys would enjoy it. I know I would."

A walk. She could do that. And she could do it without letting her mind wander back to very dangerous territory. "That sounds good. I've been cooped up inside most of the day. Besides quick trips outside for Abel, I've pretty much stayed put."

"Good. That's what Jake and I both want you to do."

"Did you two enjoy your fishing trip today?" *Did you talk about me? Does Jake think I'm as crazy as the D.C. police seem to think I am?* Those were the questions she wanted to ask, but didn't.

"It could have been better." Ben strode back into the kitchen, pulled open the drawer beneath Chloe's oven and grabbed a large frying pan.

"How so?"

"I could have caught a few edible fish." He pulled several plastic containers from the bag he'd carried in.

"You had to buy our dinner?"

"Worse." He opened the cooler and pulled out two large fish. "I had to trade for it."

"Trade?"

"Yeah. My babysitting services for Jake's fish."

"Babysitting for Jake's kids. Doesn't he have a baby and a toddler?" She was sure that was what Tiffany had said, but couldn't imagine Ben doing diaper duty.

"Yep. And unless Honor has been potty trained

sometime in the past two days, they're both still in diapers."
He pulled open a drawer, frowned, pulled open another
one. "Knives?"

"To your right."

"Thanks. Here's the problem. I'm good at a few things.
Cooking. Martial arts. Rock climbing. I'm even pretty decent
at corralling teenagers. I'm not so good at others things.
Like burping and changing babies, or playing baby doll with
a two-year-old. I'm pretty confident I can handle one of the
kids at a time, but double-duty might be beyond me."

"I'm sure you'll do just fine."

"I'm sure I'd do even better if I had another adult
there with me."

"Very subtle, Ben."

"Subtlety is my middle name." He grinned, finished
prepping the first fish and started on the second.

"And caution is mine. I might be willing to offer my help
if I knew anything at all about kids, but I don't. Besides
babysitting when I was a teenager, I haven't had much
contact with the younger crowd."

"No little brothers or sisters in your life?"

"I was my mother's first and only mistake." The words
slipped out and heat rose in Chloe's cheeks. Again.

"Sounds like your mother and mine were a lot alike."

"You said you had a sister."

"I do. My mother was too caught up in drugs and
alcohol to keep her first mistake from repeating itself.
Raven is younger than me. She and her husband live
outside of town."

"I've always wanted a sister." Someone to share the aloneness with. Someone who would be the family connection
Chloe had craved as a child and still sometimes yearned for.

"It was great. When she was little I actually did diaper duty, gave her baths, made sure she was fed."

"You were a lot older than her?"

"There's six years difference."

"That's…" Crazy. Sad. Horrifying.

"It is what it is. I took care of her the best I could until social services stepped in." He finished the second fish, opened up a shallow container and dipped both into a mixture of spices. "After that, we were separated. It took me years to find her again. And, actually, she was the one who found me. Just showed up at the church one day. I've barely let her out of my sight since."

"That's a great story."

"It is." He grinned. "I never get tired of telling it. So, what do you say?"

"About?"

"Giving me a hand with Jake's kids."

"I doubt Jake would want me over at his place."

"Why wouldn't he?"

"I'm a walking danger zone."

"And his house is like Fort Knox. Locks. Alarms. You name it, he's got it."

"His wife—"

"You've met Tiffany. She's as laid-back as Jake is intense. She'll probably feel a lot more comfortable if there are two of us with the kids."

"She did seem pretty easygoing when I met her." But that didn't mean Chloe wanted to spend the evening watching her kids. Not when doing so meant she'd be spending another evening with Ben. Ben whose vivid gaze compelled her and whose laughter warmed the cold, hard knot of pain she'd been carrying around for months. Ben who could easily fill the empty place in her heart and who could just as easily break it.

"She is, but she's also a mama bear when it comes to her kids. I doubt she'll be able to enjoy her birthday dinner if she's worrying about whether or not I'll be able to handle Honor and Isaac on my own."

"Jake is taking her out for her birthday?"

"Yes. Does that make a difference?"

"Every woman deserves to be treated special on her birthday." Chloe's own birthdays were less than memorable. Her mother and grandmother hadn't wanted to acknowledge the infamous date of her birth. Most of her boyfriends had been too caught up in themselves to mark the day. Even Adam hadn't made much of it, his quick phone calls and hasty dinner arrangements making her feel more second-thought than special. Opal had sent cards and gifts, but she was the only one who'd ever cared enough to do so.

"Does that mean you'll help?" Ben laid the fish in the sizzling hot pain and a spicy aroma filled the air.

Chloe's stomach rumbled, reminding her that she hadn't eaten since breakfast and that her mind might be fuzzy from lack of food. Now was not a good time to make decisions. She knew it, but couldn't find the wherewithal to care. "I'll help if you get Jake and Tiffany's consent first."

"That goes without saying." He nodded toward the containers he'd set on the counter. "There's corn-bread batter in the yellow container. I'll get the oven preheated. If you oil a pan and pour the batter into it, we can get it started. I don't know about you, but I'm starving."

"I could definitely eat." A horse. A house. Anything large and filling.

Chloe followed Ben's instructions, then handed him the

pan, her mouth watering as he slid it into the oven, a feeling of companionship and camaraderie washing over her. She and Adam had spent a lot of time together, but not all of it had been easy and comfortable. As a matter of fact, too much of that time had been spent arguing about his relationships with other women and Chloe's unwillingness to accept those friendships. She'd felt sure that innocent lunches and dinner would eventually turn into something less innocent. He'd insisted he loved her too much to be tempted by anyone else. In the end, Chloe's opinion regarding the matter had been proven accurate. That was cold comfort in the wake of all that had happened.

She ran her hand over already mussed hair and pulled plates out of the cupboard, hoping to distract herself from thoughts of what had been. "Is there anything else I can do to help?"

"Grab the ice cream out of the bag and throw it in the freezer. I almost forgot about it."

"Forgot about ice cream? Is that even possible?"

"Chalk it up to last-minute changes in the menu and an ornery puppy who decided he didn't want to leave the house."

"Last-minute menu changes?"

"Opal called to ask me why I'd talked you into getting a puppy."

"I haven't spoken to her since yesterday afternoon. How could she possibly know about Abel?"

"The same way anyone in Lakeview knows anything. Rumor mill. Although I'm not sure if that's an accurate description since it was your landlady who called Opal with the information."

"I had a feeling I wouldn't get much privacy living in a house owned by Opal's friend." Chloe pulled forks, knives and spoons out of a drawer, grabbed napkins from the counter and finished setting the table. "So what did Opal's lecture about Abel have to do with last-minute menu plans?"

"I haven't figured that one out yet. One minute we were talking about dogs taking over Blooming Baskets and the next she was asking me what I planned to serve tonight." He grinned, flipping the fish and opening another plastic container. "I'd been planning to have fresh fruit for dessert, but Opal told me that wouldn't do. Apparently, you need chocolate and ice cream and lots of it."

"I guess I'll have to give her a call after you leave and tell her to stop meddling."

"Do you *want* her to stop meddling?" He opened the oven, peeked at the corn bread and closed it again, leaning a hip against the counter, his eyes meeting Chloe's and capturing her gaze.

"The truth? No. Every time Opal sticks her nose into my business, I realize how much she cares."

"I feel the same about my foster parents. Mom calls every Monday. Dad checks in by e-mail a couple times a week. It's good to know they're there even if their hints about marriage and children are getting old."

"They want you to get married again?"

"They want me to be happy. I think that's what all good parents want for their children." He pulled the bread out of the oven, turned off the burner and grabbed a plate. "Ready to eat?"

"It smells delicious."

"Hopefully it will be. Of course, if it's not, I'll just blame Jake for catching bad fish."

"You two are good friends."

"He moved here from D.C. a few years back. We've

been like brothers ever since." He placed spice-crusted fish on her plate, spooned what looked like a three-bean salad from a container he pulled from the bag.

"He met Tiffany here?"

"Met her. Married her. Had a couple of kids."

"I'm surprised you haven't followed in his footsteps." The words slipped out and Chloe pressed her lips together. "Sorry, it's none of my business."

He shrugged, placed a plate in front of her. "I think a lot of people are surprised I haven't remarried, but what I had with Theresa was pretty special."

"What was she like?"

"Sweet. Soft-spoken. A little shy. Strong faith. Strong spirit. Really into homey things. Sewing. Cooking."

"She would have made a perfect pastor's wife."

"She would have, but that's not why I loved her." He sat down across from Chloe. "Unfortunately it's what just about every woman I've dated has been trying to be. I guess they all have the same idea about what it takes to be a pastor's wife."

"What's your idea?"

"My idea is that a pastor's wife should be whatever God calls her to be. Whether that means sewing, cooking, serving in church ministries, teaching. Computer forensics." He grinned, the humor in his eyes making the comment a joke rather than a promise. "We'd better eat before the puppies get restless. Do you mind if I ask the blessing?"

"Not at all."

Ben wrapped a hand around hers, his grip firm and strong as he offered a simple prayer of thanks.

This was what home should be. Not four walls and furniture, but companionship, friendship. Faith shared and expressed. The intimacy of the moment wrapped around Chloe's heart, holding it tight and promising something she shouldn't want, but did—more dinners, more quiet conversations, more Ben.

And that wasn't good at all.

As soon as Ben finished speaking, she tugged away from his hold, avoiding his deep blue gaze as she bit into the aromatic fish he'd prepared.

Ben's easy charm was nice, but there was no way she planned to fall for it. Her life was too complicated, her worries too real to waste energy and emotion on a relationship that was destined to fail the same way her other relationships had.

But what if it wasn't?

The question whispered through her mind, tempting her to believe in impossibilities, happily-ever-afters and a hundred dreams she'd buried with Adam and his betrayal.

But happily-ever-afters and dreams were for people who hadn't been deceived, people who still believed in love and all that it meant.

Chloe wasn't one of them.

FOURTEEN

They went for a walk after dinner, the two puppies tumbling along on leashes, the soft rustle of grass and the gentle lap of water against the shore filling the night. The waning moon cast a silvery glow across the dry grass, giving the world an ethereal beauty Chloe tried hard to appreciate. Tried. Despite Ben's presence, she didn't like being out after dark, the open space, the hulking trees and shadowy bushes taking on forms and faces that she was half convinced were real.

"Cold?"

She hadn't realized she was shivering until Ben spoke. At his words, she pulled her jacket closed, knowing it was fear and not the cold that had her shaking. "Maybe a little."

"Here." He shrugged off his jacket, draped it over her shoulders, the masculine outdoorsy scent of it surrounding Chloe.

"Now *you're* going to be cold."

"Not even close. My foster parents loved camping. They used to take us kids into the mountains every fall. *That* was cold. Compared to it, tonight is downright balmy." He wrapped a hand around her elbow, leading her along a sparsely covered patch of lawn, the rocks and soil treacherous under Chloe's unsteady gait.

"I've never been camping."

"Our church sponsors a youth camping trip every spring. You can sign up as chaperone and see what it's like."

"It sounds like fun, but spring is months away. Anything could happen before then."

"You think you'll move back to D.C.?"

"No, but I may not be able to stay here much longer."

"I know you're not asking for my opinion."

"But you'll give it anyway?"

He chuckled, the sound filling the night. "Something like that."

"Then I guess I'll ask. What's your opinion?"

"Trouble has a way of following us no matter how far we run from it. If we're going to have to face it anyway, we may as well face it with people who care about us."

"Maybe, but the trouble that's following me is dangerous. Not just to me, but to everyone around me. I couldn't live with myself if something happened to Opal because of me. I'd feel the same way if something happened to you, Tiffany or Jake."

"You're making our welfare your responsibility, but we can all take care of ourselves."

"That's what I thought about Adam and look what happened to him." An image filled her mind—fire, hot metal, Adam, blood seeping from his head and dripping onto the white shirt he wore.

"What happened to Adam had nothing to do with whether or not he could take care of himself. What Jackson did was unexpected. Something no one could have known to be prepared for. We're in a completely different situation now. We know there's potential danger and we're prepared for it."

"Forewarned is forearmed?"

"Exactly."

"It's not good enough, Ben. Until we find the person who's been stalking me, no one will be safe."

"Jake is working hard to find the answers we need." He turned her back toward the house. "I saw that you were working on your computer when I arrived. Dig anything up?"

"Not as much as I would have liked. I decided to look back over the cases I was working on before the accident. It's possible I've got information that I don't know I have. Something that a person might be willing to commit murder over to keep quiet."

"Maybe."

"But?"

"Someone has spent an awful lot of time trying to make it look like you're having a breakdown. I wonder why."

"Revenge?"

"That's the obvious reason, but usually acts of revenge are brutal and quick. This seems more like slow, malicious torture."

"I can't think of anyone who'd want to torture me. My clients and business acquaintances don't know me well enough to care. My friends have only been friends since I moved to D.C."

"How long ago was that?"

"Six years."

"Where were you before?"

"Chicago. I've got a few friends there that I still keep in touch with, but I can't imagine any of them wanting to harm me."

"Maybe not, but the way I see it, what's going on is really personal, more personal than just wanting to keep you out of an investigation. Maybe even more personal than wanting to pay you back for a perceived wrong. If that's true, someone you know is doing this to you."

"If someone in my life hated me that much, wouldn't I know it?"

"Not necessarily." They'd reached the porch and Ben gestured to the swing. "Want to sit for a minute?"

"If I sit, I might not be able to get back up. My leg's been giving me trouble today." Not to mention the fact that she'd had about all she could take of the darkness. Having Ben around might offer some sense of security, but a warning was crawling up her spine. Outside was not where she should be and the quicker she got back into the apartment the happier she'd be.

"Too bad, but it's probably for the best. I've got to get home. I've got a sermon to deliver in the morning. I'll walk you up to your apartment and then head out." He lifted Cain, who was racing back and forth across the porch, and pushed open the front door.

"What's your sermon about?"

"If I told you that, you'd have no reason to come hear it."

"Who said I was thinking about coming?"

"You probably weren't, but I bet you are now."

Chloe laughed. "As a matter of fact, I am."

"Good. Keep thinking about it and I'll be looking for you tomorrow." He laced his fingers through hers and led her up the stairs, waiting while she closed and locked the door.

She could hear his retreating footsteps as she collapsed into the easy chair. Hanging out with Ben had been fun, almost exhilarating, but it had done nothing to solve her problems. What it *had* done was give her something to think about. For the past few months she'd waffled between

believing a member of The Strangers was after her and believing she was coming unhinged. It hadn't occurred to her
that something completely different might be going on. Her
injuries, her grief, her surgeries had consumed her life and
left no room for much more than reaction to the circumstances she'd found herself in.

It was time to change that. To act instead of react. To start
using her skills to find the answers she needed—who? Why?

She grabbed her laptop, pulled the comforter off her bed
and settled back into the chair, flicking on the television
and letting background noise fade as she began searching
through her files once again. This time, though, she also
reread e-mails from friends and co-workers, searching for
something that would point her in the right direction and
praying that she'd know it if she saw it.

*Fire. Heat. The screaming sound of sirens. Her own
frantic cries for help choking and gasping out as she
reached for Adam's hand.* Get out. We need to get out! *The
words shrieked through her mind, but she couldn't get the
door open, couldn't find her way out of the smoke and
flames. She banged her fist against the window and saw
the shadow, leaning close, staring in at her, eyes glowing
like the flames—red and filled with hate. She screamed,
turning toward Adam, wanting desperately to wake him,
to get them both out alive. But Adam wasn't there. Instead,
she saw sandy hair, broad shoulders, a strong face covered
with blood. Blue eyes wide and lifeless.*

Ben.

Chloe screamed again, lunging up, fighting against the
seat belt and her pain. No. Not a seat belt. A blanket. Not
a car. An easy chair. Not the past. The present.

She took a deep, steadying breath and lifted Abel, who

sat whining on the floor. He felt warm and solid, his furry body comforting as Chloe stood and paced across the room. Seeing Ben in the nightmare had made it that much more terrifying, the new twist on the old dream filling her with dread.

"I need this to be over. Not tomorrow. Not the next day. Now. Before anyone else is hurt." The words were a prayer and a plea. One Chloe could only hope God heard and would answer. Anything else didn't bear thinking about.

She glanced at the clock. Four a.m. Too early to leave the house. Too late to try to get more sleep. She scratched the puppy under his chin and set him down on the floor. "How about a snack? Then we can do some more work on the computer."

Not that the hours she'd spent the previous night had revealed much. As far as she was concerned, she'd hit a dead end. She'd have to either find a way around it or take a different path.

"One that isn't as clearly connected to me. Maybe not a friend or a co-worker of mine. Maybe someone who…" What? Chloe shook her head, uncovered the plastic container of brownies Ben had left the previous night.

"I don't know who's after me, Abel, but I can tell you this—Ben's brownies are almost good enough to make me forget my worries for a while."

Almost, but not quite.

Chloe bit into the thick chocolate, poured a glass of milk, and sat down at her computer desk. Instead of logging on, she grabbed a pencil and piece of paper. Ben had given her a new possibility to consider. Were there others? Jackson was in jail, The Strangers weren't after her, she couldn't find any evidence that one of her friends or co-workers had an axe to grind with her. What else was there? Who else was there?

Adam's friends? His co-workers?

He'd been acting odd in the month before they broke up. After he'd confessed to seeing someone else, Chloe had chalked his behavior up to guilt and stress. Could something else have caused it?

She jotted a note down on the paper, wishing she could pick up the phone and call Ben, discuss the idea with him.

"Scratch that thought. I don't need to call Ben. I don't need to discuss my idea with him. I've got you to talk to, buddy." She bent down to stroke Abel's soft fur. "And a plate of brownies to devour."

But brownies were a poor substitute for human company and conversation, and Chloe figured she'd trade a brownie or two for someone willing to listen to her at this time of the morning.

She sighed, pacing across the floor, pulling back the curtains on the balcony door. The darkness beyond the window was complete, the moon already set, the stars hidden behind thick clouds. Soon it would be dawn, but until then, Chloe was alone, waiting for the darkness to disappear and for the bright light of day to pull her completely out of the nightmare.

FIFTEEN

It had been weeks since Chloe had been to church and she almost decided to skip it again, her throbbing head and aching leg protesting the hours spent in front of the computer. Only the thought of having to explain her absence to Opal got her in the shower, dressed and out the door. The church parking lot was nearly full when she arrived, the sanctuary buzzing with people as she moved down the aisle and found a seat near the back. Maybe if she was lucky, she'd go unnoticed, though based on the number of people who were looking her way, she doubted it.

"I *thought* that was your beat-up old Mustang in the parking lot. You should have called me. We could have ridden here together." Opal slid into the pew beside Chloe, hair bouncing around her square face, her dark gaze shrewd. "Everything go okay last night? You look a little pale."

"It was fine."

"Fine? You spent the evening with one of Lakeview's most eligible bachelors and all you can manage to say is that it was fine?"

"The food was wonderful."

"And the company?"

"Wonderful, too."

"I knew it."

"Knew what?"

"That you and Ben would hit it off. Now, tell me why you're so pale."

"I didn't sleep well."

"Because?"

"My leg's been bothering me." That was as much of the truth as she was prepared to give.

"You've got an appointment with the doctor this week, right?"

"Yes."

"Well, make sure you tell him how much trouble you're having. I don't like the way you've been limping around."

"I fractured my femur and crushed my knee, Opal. The pain from that isn't going to go away."

"I know, but I still don't like it." She sighed, her flowery perfume nearly choking Chloe as she leaned close and patted her hand. "I'm glad you're here this morning. I didn't think any of my children would settle close to home. I'm glad one finally had the good sense to move back."

"Really? One of the girls is planning to move here?" Chloe couldn't help hoping that Opal's third daughter Anna was the one who would be returning. Five years older than Chloe, she'd been a good role model and friend when they were kids.

"I'm talking about you." Opal huffed the words, her disgust obvious. "That you didn't realize that wounds me deeply, Chloe."

"Wounds you deeply? I think we're heading for a guilt trip. Which means you want something from me."

Opal chuckled, her hand wrapping around Chloe's, the skin, once smooth and pale, now wrinkled and spotted with age. Still, her grip was firm, her eyes bright. "You know me too well, my dear. I do have a favor to ask."

"Do you need me to open the store for you tomorrow?"

"No, nothing like that. I've decided to go…" she glanced around, her broad, strong face flushing pink "…on the senior singles trip."

"Senior singles trip?"

"To Richmond for a few days of shopping and fun. Our Sunday school has been planning the trip for a while. I figure since I had to cut my visit with Elizabeth short when Jenna went into labor, I deserve a few days off."

"It sounds like fun."

"It will be, but I'll be gone Thursday through Sunday. Mary Alice is going to work full time those days. Between you, her and Laura we should be okay."

"So what do you need me to do?"

"Can you bring my mail in the house and check on Checkers?"

"Checkers does not need to be checked on. He can fend for himself just fine."

"Checkers is a sweet cat once you get to know him. He just needs a lot of love."

"And a pound of flesh." Chloe had been to Opal's house one time since her return to Lakeview and during the visit she'd been attacked by a very fat, very grumpy black-and-white cat.

"He barely touched you, Chloe. I'd think a young woman whose rearing I had a hand in would be too tough to complain about a tiny little scratch." Opal turned her attention to the pulpit and the choir that was filling the loft.

"It was more than a scratch, but I'll take care of Checkers anyway."

"Maybe I did raise you right after all." Opal smiled. "Just remember, Checkers is sweet, but he's finicky. He likes his dinner served at six o'clock on the dot. No sooner. No later."

Six o'clock in November meant being out past sundown. The thought filled Chloe with trepidation and she wiped a damp palm against her black skirt. "It might be better if I feed him in the afternoon. Maybe during my lunch break."

"The last time I went away Anna was in town. She put Checker's food in the bowl in the morning and he refused to touch it. I'd hate to think of him going hungry for four days."

Chloe sighed. "All right. I'll feed him at six. Was there something else you needed me to do?"

"I need to go shopping and I need a fashion expert to come with me."

"Fashion expert? For a trip to Richmond?"

"I've got a date Friday night." Opal's cheeks went pink again and Chloe couldn't help smiling.

"A date with Sam?"

"If it's any of your business, yes."

"Good for you, Opal."

"So you'll come shopping?"

"I'm not a fashion expert."

"You're the closest thing I've got. What do you say? It'll only be for a few hours tomorrow night."

"What time?"

"As soon as we close the store."

"Sounds good." It would sound better if they were going during the day, but Chloe didn't have the heart to say no.

"Wonderful. We'll have dinner, spend a few hours clothes shopping, and—" Before she could complete the thought the call to worship began and the before-church chatter ceased.

That worked for Chloe.

The noisy prattle of the sanctuary had done nothing to ease her pounding headache or offer her relief from the tension she'd been feeling all morning. She'd come hoping to find some small sense of peace. All she'd found were more worries. The thought of taking care of Checkers, of driving to Opal's house at night, filled her with a sick dread. Going shopping after dark didn't make her any happier. The fact that either bothered her only made Chloe even more conscious of just how much her life had changed in the past eleven months.

The music faded and Ben strode to the pulpit, his long legs and broad shoulders showcased to perfection in a dark suit and light blue shirt. His words were strong, but not dramatic as he welcomed the congregation, prayed, then stepped aside so that the music minister could lead the first song. Chloe knew her attention should be on the man leading the music, but instead it was drawn to Ben again and again. His smile seemed to encompass the room, his eyes even more vivid in the bright light that streamed in through tall windows.

He scanned the sanctuary, his gaze traveling the room. There was no way he could see Chloe in the midst of the crowd, but somehow he found her, his eyes meeting hers, his lips quirking in a half smile that made her treacherous heart dance a jig.

"Are you going to sing, or just stand there gawking at Ben?" Opal elbowed Chloe in the side, her quiet hiss forcing Chloe's attention away from the man who'd been taking up too many of her thoughts during the past few days.

"I wasn't gawking." She'd been looking. Maybe even staring. But she hadn't been gawking.

"Good to know. Now sing before someone notices that you're not. I don't want to spend the entire ride to Richmond answering questions about your disinterest in music."

"No one's noticing, Opal."

"*Everyone's* noticing. Now, sing."

Chloe managed to do as Opal suggested without glancing at Ben again. By the time he stood up to deliver the sermon, the tension and anxiety that had accompanied her through the long predawn hours had finally eased, the familiar hymns and sweet sounds of voices joining in praise accomplishing what no amount of alone-time could.

When Ben finally spoke, his words about faith in the midst of crisis spoke to her soul, the message echoing the quiet yearning that had brought her back to her Bible again and again over the past few days. She might not understand God's plan or His will, but she had to trust that He would work His best in her life.

The sermon ended and Chloe stood for the final hymn, the quick movement making her lightheaded. She grabbed the front of the pew, holding herself steady as she tried to blink the darkness from the edges of her vision.

"Are you okay? You've gone white as a sheet." Opal touched her arm, true concern etching lines around her eyes and mouth.

"Fine. I just stood up too quickly."

Opal's lips tightened and she shook her head. "A little dizzy? Sit down. Put your head between your knees."

"That won't be necessary. I'm completely recovered."

"Are you sure? Maybe I should drive you home."

"And then have to come pick me up for work tomorrow? I don't think so."

"Chloe—"

"Opal, I'm fine. I promise."

Opal looked like she wanted to argue, but raising four kids must have taught her when to fight and when to let go. "All right, but if you get out to your car and change your mind let me know."

"I will."

"I'll call you this evening to finalize plans for my trip to Richmond."

"To check up on me, you mean."

"That, too. Now, I'd better go see if I can find Sam so I can let him know I'm definitely going on the trip." She leaned over and kissed Chloe's cheek. "Be good, my dear. And be careful."

"I will be."

Opal merged into the crowd that was exiting the sanctuary while Chloe held back, waiting until the room emptied and just a few clusters of people remained. When she was sure her limping progress wouldn't block anyone's exit, she stepped out into the aisle and headed to door.

"Chloe, I was hoping I'd see you here." Brian McMath stepped up beside her, his slim, runner's frame dressed to perfection in a dark suit and staid tie.

"Brian. It's good to see you again." And would remain good as long as he didn't mention her scars again.

"I'm glad you feel that way. I've been thinking about the conversation we had the other day and I wanted to apologize if I came on too strong. I hope my interest in your scars and the medical treatment of them didn't make you uncomfortable." Coming from another doctor, the words might have sounded sincere. Coming from Brian McMath, they sounded phony and well-practiced.

"I appreciate your apology."

"Good. Then maybe you'll let me make things up to you. How about having lunch with me?" They stepped out of the sanctuary and headed toward the exit.

"I'm sorry, I can't."

"You have plans?"

"Yes." She planned to take Abel for a walk. Maybe take a nap.

"With Opal?"

Obviously, Brian wasn't going to give up. Chloe was about to tell him exactly what she had planned and why she wasn't going to disrupt those plans for him, when they stepped out into watery light and she saw Ben.

He looked great standing on the church steps, his hair curling around his collar, his relaxed confidence appealing. He must have sensed her gaze because he looked up, his half smile becoming a full-out grin as she approached.

"I thought I saw you sitting beside Opal. I'm glad you came." His hand was warm as he clasped it around hers, pulling her a step closer, his gaze settling on Brian. "I'm glad you're here, too, Brian. I hear things were hectic at the hospital this weekend. I thought maybe you'd be caught up in a case there."

"I don't believe in working on Sunday, pastor. I'm sure you know me well enough to know that."

"I'm sure I do." Ben smiled again, but Chloe had the distinct impression he didn't really care for the doctor or his comments.

Brian nodded, then turned to Chloe. "Since we're not going to be able to have lunch today, I'm going to take off. Maybe I'll see you at the quilting circle this Wednesday." He strode away before Chloe could comment and she wasn't sorry to see him leave.

"You're smiling. I guess that means you're glad to see him go."

"He's a little overwhelming."

"Good choice of words. So, maybe since you're not having lunch with Brian, you'd like to come over to my place and have lunch with me."

"Abel won't be happy if I leave him home alone much longer."

"You can bring him over."

"I don't want to put you out." She also didn't want to say no. No matter how much she knew she should.

"I've got beef stew and homemade rolls already made. More than enough for two people."

She really *should* refuse. Chloe knew it. But even as she was telling herself that she should stay away from Ben she was opening her mouth to agree. "Beef stew and rolls sound good. I can bring what's left of the brownies over for dessert."

"Sounds good. I'll meet you over at my place in fifteen minutes or so."

"See you then." Chloe limped down the steps and got in her car, sure that she was making a mistake. Allowing Ben into her life was dangerous for both of them. Chloe had already had her heart broken once, she had no intention of letting it happen again. But what bothered her more than thoughts of heartbreak was the dream—the image of Ben broken and lifeless in the front seat of a burning car.

Just thinking about it made her shudder. Sure Ben could take care of himself. Sure he was capable and strong, but Adam had been, too, and despite what Ben had said the previous night, Chloe couldn't help worrying.

She stepped out of the car and started up the porch

steps, a flash of movement to the left catching her attention. She turned, her pulse leaping, her heart racing. She wasn't sure what she expected to see, but the small ball of fluff that was rushing toward her wasn't it. "Abel?"

She scooped the puppy up into her arms, fear burning a path down her throat and settling deep in her stomach. "How'd you get out here?"

She asked, but she really didn't want to know, didn't want to imagine someone opening her apartment door while she was gone, didn't want to think that someone might still be there. Instead, she stumbled back toward her car, locked herself inside, hesitating with her hand on the phone. She hadn't crated Abel before she'd left. Was it possible he'd snuck out the door while she was leaving? Slipped down the stairs and out the door without her notice?

Maybe.

Or maybe someone had broken into her apartment and inadvertently let him out. She could call the police. She could go see if her apartment door was open.

She could sit here all day trying to decide what to do.

She rubbed the puppy's fur, wishing she didn't have so much doubt in her ability to know real danger from imagined. She didn't want to call the police and look like a fool. She didn't want to not call if something was really going on. Abel growled a deep warning that made the hair on the back of Chloe's neck stand on end. She scanned the driveway, the yard, the trees. The porch.

She froze, watching in horror as the door she'd left closed slowly began to open.

SIXTEEN

Ben hadn't planned on inviting Chloe to lunch. Then again, he hadn't planned on seeing her at church. When he'd glanced around the sanctuary and caught sight of her, the jolt of awareness he'd felt was an unexpected surprise.

"I don't know what your plans are, Lord, but I sure would like to. Chloe's not the kind of woman I can be just friends with. If that's all You've got planned for us, I'm not sure I'm up for the task."

Cain barked, his feet slipping on tile as he raced through the kitchen and parked himself in front of the front door.

"Are they here?" Ben strode across the room and nudged Cain out of the way as a soft tap sounded on the wood. "Hi…"

The greeting died on his lips as he caught sight of Chloe, her face white, the few freckles that dusted the bridge of her nose standing out in sharp contrast.

He pulled her into the house, his hands skimming down thin arms and coming to rest on her waist. She was shaking, her breath coming in short, quick gasps. "Hey, are you okay?"

"Yes. No." A tear rolled down her cheek, and she swiped it away, the gesture abrupt and filled with irritation.

"What's wrong?"

"Everything." She sniffed back more tears, pacing across the room, her limp pronounced, her posture stiff.

"That covers a lot of bases, Chloe."

"It does, doesn't it?"

"What happened?" He urged her around to face him. Her eyes were deep emerald and filled with stark emotion. Anger. Frustration. Not the fear or sadness he'd expected to see.

"Just one more piece of evidence proving that I'm as unhinged as the D.C. police think."

"No one thinks you're unhinged."

"No, they just believe my imagination is working overtime. The worst part is, they're right."

"You've got a reason for saying that. Why don't you tell me?"

"Abel was outside when I got home from church. I hadn't left him out there."

Ben's hand tightened on Chloe's shoulder and he had to force his grip to ease. "Did you call Jake?"

"I was going to. I got in my car and grabbed the phone, but my downstairs neighbor came out before I made the call. I guess Abel was hanging out in the foyer. Connor thought he was a stray and put him outside. He was very apologetic."

She paused, a smile chasing away some of her irritation. "The fact that I was having a panic attack when he came outside sent him into fits of remorse. He wanted to call an ambulance, but I told him I'd be fine once I stopped hyperventilating."

She was making light of the situation, but Ben knew it had bothered her a lot more than she was saying. "I'm sure he'll get over the trauma eventually. Did you ever call Jake?"

"So he could come and tell me that Abel slipped out of

the house while I was leaving?" She raked a hand through her hair and shook her head. "No way. I've been through that kind of embarrassment one too many times."

"I think it's better to be a little embarrassed than a lot dead." The words were harsher than he'd meant them and Chloe stiffened, the color that had slowly returned to her face gone again.

"Connor went up to the apartment with me. It was locked up tight. No sign that anyone had been there. Nothing out of the ordinary."

"That's how your apartment was when we found the photos on your digital camera and how it was when you overdosed on pain medication you've said you didn't take." His words were hard, ground out through gritted teeth and frustration. Chloe was a intelligent, strong woman. The fact that she seemed to *want* to believe that she was imagining things was something he couldn't understand.

"But this time nothing happened. No weird photos. No missing medicine."

"How do you know, Chloe? Did you check every container in your refrigerator? Make sure the furnace hadn't been tampered with? We need to call Jake and let him do what he does best—look for evidence."

"And when he finds nothing, I'll be right back where I started—struggling to figure out what's going on while everyone around me insists that nothing is."

"You'll never be back where you started." He smoothed the bangs out of her eyes, silky strands of hair catching on his rough palms. "You have people here who believe in you. That's not going to change."

"Won't it? What if this stuff goes on for a month? Two months? Don't you think Jake is going to get a little tired of running to my rescue when there's nothing to rescue me from?"

"There's something to rescue you from, Chloe. Just because we don't know what that is yet, doesn't mean it isn't real. Jake knows that. I know that. Neither of us are going to give up until we find the person responsible for everything that's happened to you."

She smiled, moving away from his touch, her hair sliding over his knuckles, the dark strands falling over her shoulders and covering the scars on her neck. What she'd been through couldn't be hidden, though. It lived in her eyes and her voice. "I think I know that, but I still don't want to go through the same thing I went through in D.C., feeling sure something terrible was going to happen only to have the police prove me wrong every time."

"They didn't prove you wrong. They just never proved you right. That's what we're going to do and the first step is letting Jake take a look at your apartment."

"He can look, but you're the one who's going to take responsibility if he decides it was a big waste of his time."

"Jake's philosophy is better safe than sorry. I feel the same." Ben picked up the phone and dialed Jake's home number, antsy to get things moving. No way did he believe Chloe had let Abel out of the apartment without realizing it. If she hadn't let the puppy out, someone else had. The sooner they discovered what that person had been doing in her apartment, the better Ben would feel.

"Reed here."

"Jake, it's Ben."

"What's up?"

"We've got a situation. I thought you might like to check it out."

"Tell me."

Ben gave Jake the details, knowing his friend would be as anxious to find out what was going on as he was.

"I'll be at your house in fifteen minutes. If Chloe gives me the key, I can go back to her apartment and check things out."

"Thanks."

"What did he say?" Chloe leaned against the wall, her posture deceptively relaxed, the anxiety she'd managed to harness showing only in her white-knuckled fists.

"He'll be here in fifteen minutes to get your keys. He wants to check things out."

"There won't be any evidence to lead him in the right direction. There never is."

"This time might be different."

"Or it might be the same as every other time." She smiled, but the frustration in her eyes was unmistakable. "I'm ready for the nightmare to be over, but no matter how hard I look, I can't see any ending to it."

"There's an ending to it. It may take time, but we'll find it." Ben pulled her forward, wrapping his arms around her waist. She leaned her head against his chest, her hair tickling his chin, a subtle floral scent drifting on the air. He wanted to inhale deeply, take it into his lungs and savor it. Memorize it so that in five years, ten, twenty, he'd remember standing in his house with Chloe, staring out over the parsonage yard, realizing…

What?

That it felt right, good, *permanent.* That there was going to be much more to their relationship than either of them expected or even wanted.

He shoved aside the thought, but didn't move away

from Chloe. Partly because holding her *did* feel right, partly because she seemed to need his support.

Her hands rested on his waist, her body not stiff, but not relaxed, either. As if she didn't want to allow herself to get too close. And maybe she didn't. She'd been through a lot with Adam. Keeping her distance might be the only way she felt she could keep her heart intact.

"You're right about it taking time to find the answers, Ben." She spoke quietly, lifting her head so that she could meet his gaze, her eyes the color of spring's promise, but filled with the starkness of winter. "That's exactly what I'm worried about. Time. I think it's running out."

He wished he could tell her she was wrong, but he felt the same way. Time wasn't on their side and the longer it took for them to track down Chloe's stalker, the more likely it was that that person would act again. Maybe next time with more serious results. "God is in control, *not* the person who's stalking you. It's His timing, His will that's going to be done. We can take comfort in that."

"Maybe so, but right now it seems like a cold comfort." She frowned, stepped out of his arms. "I've been a Christian since I was fifteen. I *know* God will work things out in His time and His way. I just wish I knew what that meant for my life."

"I think that's the hardest thing about faith, Chloe. Trusting the driver even when we can't clearly see the road He's taking us on."

"Oh, I can see the road all right. It's covered with ice and has a hundred-foot drop on either side."

Ben chuckled, smoothing his hands over Chloe's silky hair, framing her face with his palms. "If God's the driver, you don't have to worry about going over the edge."

"Maybe that's the problem. Maybe I've been doing most of the driving these past few years."

"If that's the case, you'd better take it slow and drive carefully."

"You're not going to tell me I should get out of the driver's seat?" She raised a dark eyebrow, the smile that curved her lips softening the sharp line of her jaw.

"I didn't think you'd want to hear me say something you already know."

"I do know it, but doing it isn't always as easy as it should be. I like plans. I like purpose. I like to know where I'm headed." She turned to stare out the window, her gaze fixed on some distant point. A thought. A memory. Something sad and ugly from the look in her eyes.

He wrapped an arm around her waist, tugging her back against his chest, wanting to offer comfort, but not sure that words could touch the hurt that Chloe tried so hard to hide. "There is a plan, you know. And a purpose. Whether you see it or not."

She nodded, her hair brushing against his chin, the silky strands reminding him of long-ago days, of femininity and softness, sweet smiles and gentle laughter. It had been a long time since he'd had any of those things in his life. Today, with Chloe in his arms and the gray-gold beauty of autumn outside the window, he missed them more than he had since the first days following Theresa's death.

That meant something and he couldn't ignore it. If there was one thing he'd learned from watching Theresa live, watching her die, it was that life was too short to waste time, to make excuses, to turn away from what God willed and wanted. His wife had embraced every challenge, every problem with open arms and an open heart. She hadn't let fear stop her, hadn't let her disease keep her from the things she felt called to do. Her example had set the course for much of Ben's life in the years since he'd buried her.

And it would set his course now.

If this was what God had planned for his life, if *Chloe* was, he wouldn't turn his back on it.

His arm tightened a fraction on her waist and he pulled her a little closer. One way or another, he had a feeling that with Chloe things were going to get a whole lot worse before they got better.

SEVENTEEN

Jake arrived less than fifteen minutes after Ben called him, his face set in hard lines, his long legs eating up the ground as he paced Ben's living room. He didn't look happy and Chloe figured that could only mean bad news.

"I just got a call from a friend on the Arlington police force. He heard I was checking into your case and thought I might be interested in knowing that your fiancé had filed a crime report a few months before he was killed. Did you know that?"

"Yes. It didn't seem like a big deal at the time. Someone broke into his apartment, took a watch, a tie and cuff links. A few dollar bills he'd left lying on his dresser."

"It didn't seem like a big deal at the time, but now it does?"

"I was thinking about things last night. Ben had asked me if I'd felt stalked before the accident. The weeks leading up to it are blurry, but I don't recall anything strange happening. To me."

"But things *were* happening to Adam?" Jake pulled his notebook out, started writing. "What besides the break-in?"

"What are you thinking, Jake?" Ben lounged near the door, his shoulder against the wall, his thick hair mussed.

"I'm thinking there may be a connection between the

break-in and the accident. I'm thinking that maybe Adam is that connection. That he was the intended victim, not Chloe."

"I wondered that, too, but why try to kill Adam by sabotaging *my* car?"

"Good question. I don't have an answer yet, but I plan to find one." Jake paced back across the room, paused in front of Chloe, his dark blue eyes staring into hers. "Do you have any ideas? Anything that didn't seem important at the time, but that seems like it might be connected now."

"Yes."

"You answered pretty quickly."

"Like I said, I was thinking about it last night. I planned to call you tomorrow."

"You should have called me this morning."

"What's done is done, Jake. Let's move on from here." Ben seemed completely at ease, but Chloe sensed a tension in him that belied his relaxed posture.

"Good point." Jake's sharp gaze was still on Chloe "So, tell me what you thought of last night."

"Not much, just some little things that didn't seem related when I looked at them separately. Once I started connecting the dots, they seemed to make a cohesive picture."

"Go ahead."

"A week or so before we broke up, Adam had his cell phone and home phone number changed. He said he was getting too many crank calls."

"Did you ask him what he meant?"

"Yes. He didn't give me a lot of details. Just said he was getting a lot of hang ups during the day and in the middle of the night. Once he had the number changed everything seemed fine."

She hesitated, then continued. "After I found out he'd been seeing someone else, I figured the calls had been from his girlfriend and put the issue out of my mind."

"Anything else?"

"Nothing definitive. Just a sense I had that something was wrong. In the months before we broke up, even in the weeks after, Adam didn't seem himself."

"He was seeing another woman and hiding it from you. Once you did find out, you broke up with him. I think that's a good reason to not be himself."

"That's what I thought, but Adam didn't believe in dwelling on things. Whether it was his mistake or someone else's, he was always quick to forgive and move on. Maybe I'm wrong, but when I think back, it seems like he was worried. Maybe even scared. And that wasn't like Adam at all."

"Looking backward at something doesn't often give us a clear picture." But as he spoke, Jake was scribbling in his notebook.

"Maybe not, but I've struggled to think of a reason someone would want to hurt me. If the stalker is after me because of The Strangers case, why the slow torture? Why not just do what Jackson did and get it over with quickly? If he's trying to keep me from discovering information hidden in one of the computers I was working on before the accident, he succeeded. I quit my job. Moved away. Why keep coming after me and risk being found out?

"You're making good points."

"They're Ben's not mine, but they make sense."

"They do and they're leading in the direction I've been thinking this case was going—if we're going to find your stalker we need to start looking at people who knew your fiancé, who were close to him, who might have had something to gain from his death and yours."

"Everyone loved Adam. I can't imagine someone wanting to hurt him."

"Someone did hurt him. It's time to find out who. When I get back to the office, I'm going to call and see if any evidence was collected from Adam's apartment after the break-in, and I'm going to see if I can get copies of phone records for his two old numbers. Maybe we'll find a pattern of calls, match a number and name to it. You make a list of Adam's friends and co-workers. And see if you can track down the name of the woman he was seeing."

"His business partner might be able to tell me. James and Adam went to high school together. They were like brothers."

"Then that's where you should start. I'm going to head over to your apartment and do the preliminary walk-through. You can meet me there in a half hour and we'll go through the place together."

He stepped out the door and drove away, leaving Chloe alone with Ben again. She wasn't sure how she felt about that. In the moments before Jake had arrived, she'd stood with Ben's arm wrapped around her waist, his breath ruffling her hair, the comfort of his presence making her want to lean back against his chest, accept his support. His strength.

She hadn't, but that was more a matter of timing than willpower. If Jake hadn't arrived and broken the silence that seemed filled with dreams and hopes, Chloe might have caved in to temptation, allowed herself to lean on Ben for a just a little while.

And that would have been a disaster. A little while with Ben could never be enough.

"Did you love him?" Ben's question pulled Chloe from her thoughts and she met his eyes, saw sympathy and concern in his gaze.

Had she loved Adam?

For a while she'd thought so, his attentiveness, humor and gregarious personality a perfect foil for her own more serious nature. Things had changed though, the excitement of new love fading. Or maybe the relationship hadn't changed as much as Chloe's perception of it had. She'd wanted to be first, not second, a necessity rather than an extra, a vital part of Adam's life rather than one more person to spend time with. She wanted so much more than what Adam wanted to give.

"I thought I did, but I don't think I knew what love really was."

"And you do now?"

"Now I know what it isn't."

"What's that?"

"Physical attraction, a sudden thrill of emotion when you see the person walk into the room." She shrugged. "In the end, I wanted more than that. Loyalty. Friendship. Shared goals and dreams. Maybe I wanted too much."

"I don't think you wanted any more than what you deserve." Ben was standing so close Chloe could see the flecks of silver in his eyes, could smell the woodsy fragrance that clung to him, feel the heat of his body warming the air around her.

She stepped back, swallowing past her suddenly dry throat. Everything she'd wanted from Adam, everything he couldn't give, she could see in Ben's eyes.

That wasn't good. At all.

She started toward the front door, wanting to put

distance between them. "It must be time to go over to my house now."

"Why? Am I making you uncomfortable?"

"Not at all."

He grinned, a slow deliberate curving of his lips, his eyes flashing with humor. "Could have fooled me. But you're right, we'd better get going. Grab your pup. I'll grab mine and we'll head out."

"You don't have to come."

"Is that the same as, 'I don't want you to come'?"

She wanted to say yes, but couldn't get the word past her lips. How could it be that in just over a week of knowing the man, he'd become such a big part of her life? She shook her head, lifting Abel and carrying him toward the door. "No. It's the same as 'You don't have to come.'"

He smiled, looped an arm through hers. "In that case, I think I'll tag along."

Ben's cell phone rang before they could walk out the door. "Give me a minute to get this. It might be an emergency."

He lifted the phone, frowning as he glanced at the caller ID. "It's Jake. He must have found something."

Chloe tensed, not sure what Jake was going to say, but pretty certain it wouldn't be good.

"Hello? Yeah, we're still at my place." He met Chloe's eyes, the heat of his gaze spearing through Chloe.

She paced across the room, her heart beating a hard, fast rhythm. She told herself it was from fear, that worry over what Jake had to say was causing her pulse to race, but she knew that was only part of the truth.

"I'll ask her. Chloe?"

She turned to face Ben again, steeling herself against the force of his gaze and for whatever he had to say. "Yes?"

"Whose photo was on your dresser?"

"No one's. I've got photographs hanging on my wall, but nothing on my dresser."

Ben relayed the information to Jake, listened for a moment, then nodded. "We'll be there in ten."

He hung up the phone and pulled open the door, gesturing for Chloe to step outside. "Jake found a photograph on your dresser. A picture of a man and woman. Both their heads have been cut out of the photo. You didn't see it when you got home this afternoon?"

"I didn't walk through the apartment. I just grabbed Abel's leash and the brownies and left. Since the door was locked, I assumed no one had been there."

"Someone was. Who has the key besides you?"

"My landlady. Opal. That's it."

"Who would have had access to it?"

"No one."

"Then whoever it was got in some other way. Let's get over to your place and see what Jake is thinking."

Chloe stepped outside, the cool overcast day doing nothing to reassure her as she hurried to her car and pulled open the door. Ben stopped her before she got in, his hand on her arm, his expression grim. "When we get to your place, Jake is going to ask a lot of questions. He comes off as gruff, but he means well."

"I get that about him."

"Good, because if you've got any idea who might be behind this, you need to tell him. No matter how unlikely you think it is. Any clue. Any detail you remember that might seem insignificant. He needs to know it all if he's going to be able to help you."

"If I had any idea who was behind what's been going

on, I would have told the D.C. police." She shoved her bangs out of her eyes, disgusted to realize her hand was shaking. "But I'll answer his questions the best way I can. I'm as anxious as he is to get this all over with."

"It'll be over soon." Ben pulled her into a brief hug before he started toward his car. "I'll follow you to your place."

Chloe climbed into the Mustang and pulled out onto the road, her stomach churning with nerves. When she was in D.C. she'd been desperate for someone to believe in her. Now she had two people standing beside her, doing everything they could to help her. Three if she counted Opal. That should have made her feel better. Instead, it increased her worry.

"But I'm not going to worry. I'm going to act. The answers are somewhere. I just have to find them." She muttered the words and Abel barked, as though agreeing.

She absently patted his head, her mind racing ahead. To the apartment. To the conversation she was about to have with Jake. To what needed to be done to find out who might have wanted to hurt Adam. Who was still trying to hurt Chloe.

"Lord, I'm going to need your help on this in a big way. The path I'm on is treacherous, but I know you can steer me to safety."

The prayer whispered through her mind as Chloe pulled up in front of the Victorian and stepped out of the car, waiting for Ben to do the same.

EIGHTEEN

Jake was waiting in her apartment, a silver frame held in gloved hands. She knew the picture even before she got close enough to see it. The old-fashioned silver frame was one she'd bought from an antique dealer in Georgetown, the Victorian scrolling and fine details easily recognizable.

"I found this on your dresser. Is it yours?" As Ben had predicted, Jake's words were as gruff as ever, his gaze hard.

"Yes. It's our engagement picture. We had it taken a few weeks after Adam proposed. I couldn't make myself throw it away. I gave it to Adam's parents before I moved." She leaned close, blanching as she caught sight of the photograph.

Adam's face had been cut out, leaving a neat oval where his head had been. Chloe's image had fared even worse. It looked like someone had taken a razor blade and sliced through that side of the photo over and over again.

"Call them. See what they did with it."

It wasn't a request and Chloe didn't even consider arguing. Her heart was pounding as she lifted the phone and dialed the familiar number.

"Hello?" The once vibrant voice of Karen Mitchell sounded weak and quiet, as if losing her only son had sapped some of her own life.

"Karen? It's Chloe."

"Chloe! How are you feeling, dear?"

"Fine. I just—"

"Then you're over your cold? I'm glad. You've been through so much this past year. Did the picture arrive in one piece?"

"Picture?" Chloe's hand tightened around the phone, her heart racing so fast she was sure she it would jump out of her chest.

"Your engagement photo. That is what you wanted me to send, isn't it?"

"Karen, I didn't ask you send the engagement picture. I didn't ask you to send anything."

"Dear, you called me last week and asked me to send it to you."

"No, I—"

Jake shook his head, a sharp, quick gesture that stalled the words in Chloe's throat. "Ask her where she sent it."

"Karen, listen, can you give me the address you sent the photo to?"

"So it didn't arrive? What a shame. I know how much the picture means to you."

"Do you have the address I gave you?"

"Of course. It's right in my address book." Papers rustled, Karen's words carrying over the sound and the throbbing pulse of Chloe's terror. "Here it is." She rattled off the address, a PO box that Chloe didn't recognize.

She wrote it down, her hand trembling, the letters and numbers wobbly and unclear. "Okay. Thanks."

"Is everything all right, dear? You don't seem yourself."

"Everything is fine. Listen, I was wondering if you still had Adam's laptop."

Jake raised an eyebrow at the question, but kept silent as she continued the conversation.

"Not his laptop. Jordyn said it belonged to the business. I do have his other computer, though. It's in the spare room with his other things. I haven't had the heart to go through everything."

"I understand. And I hate to even bring this up, but I'd really like to take a look at the computer. Can I send you the money to have it shipped here?"

Karen was silent for a moment. When she spoke, her voice was stronger than it had been. "Is something going on, Chloe?"

"I'm not sure. I'm hoping that Adam's computer might help me figure it out."

"I'll send it to you then. Shall I ship it to the same address?"

"No. Send it to this one." Chloe rattled off her address and phone number, then hung up, her pulse racing with anticipation and with fear.

"Asking for the computer was good thinking. If Adam was having trouble with someone, there may be evidence of that on his computer." Ben was holding Abel, his strong hand smoothing the puppy's long fur.

"That's what I'm hoping."

"What *I'm* hoping," Jake interrupted their conversation. "Is that our perpetrator's mistake will be to our benefit."

"Mistake?" In Chloe's estimation, her stalker had made far too few of those.

"The PO box. He had to have known how easily he could be traced through it."

"Maybe he didn't care." Ben sat on the couch, stretching his long legs, looking as if he belonged there.

"Or she." Jake leaned a shoulder against the wall, his

brow creasing. "Someone was impersonating Chloe. It would be hard for a man to sound like a woman."

"A woman." Chloe rolled the words across her tongue, testing them out. "That would make sense."

"Hell hath no fury like a woman scorned." Jake muttered the words, his gaze on the photo. "And based on the way you've been carved out of this photo, I'm thinking someone definitely felt scorned."

"All we need to do is find out who." Chloe glanced at the photo again.

"Any ideas?"

"No, but the answer may lie in Adam's computers. Karen's going to send me his PC. I'll see if I can get James's permission to take a look at his laptop. E-mails. Old files. There may be a name there somewhere. If there is, I'll find it."

"Good. While you do that, I'll check into phone records and get information on our PO box owner."

"How long will that take?" Ben asked the question that was foremost in Chloe's mind.

"A few days, but getting the information is no guarantee we'll find our stalker. It's unlikely our perp is using a real name. In the long run, that won't matter. We're going to find our quarry. It's only a matter of time." Jake placed the framed photo in an evidence bag, sealed it closed. "I've already dusted for prints and checked to see if the locks on the balcony or front door were jimmied."

"Were they?" Chloe would rather think someone had jimmied her door than spend hours worrying that someone had her key.

"Not that I could see, but it wouldn't take much to open your front door. A credit card would probably do it."

"I thought that was only in the movies."

"No. It's a pretty simple thing to do once you know how. It's probably a good idea if you get new locks and bolts installed."

"I can call someone tomorrow."

"Or we can take care of it today." Ben stood and strode to the balcony door. "This one needs a bolt, too."

"I'm on the second floor."

"And your neighbors are gone more than they're home. It wouldn't be hard for someone to use a ladder to gain access to your apartment."

"Ben's right. It doesn't make sense to take chances. I'm going to get back to the office and run the prints I've found. Make a few phone calls. I'll be sending patrol cars down this way every hour or so until we get this case solved."

"I appreciate it."

"Just be careful and watch your back." Jake strode out the door and Ben started after him.

"I'm going to run to the hardware store and go home for some tools. Then I'll be back. Keep the door bolted until then."

"I've got tools."

"What kind?"

"What do you need?" Chloe hurried to her room and pulled a small toolbox from her closet, setting it on the bed and opening it.

"That looks pretty complete. I don't suppose you have spare locks in there."

"Spare locks aren't on the list of things a single woman needs to keep in her house."

"But pink hammers are?" He lifted the tool, smiling a little as he hefted the weight in his hand.

"Just because it's pink doesn't mean it's not functional."

"I'm sure it's functional. I'm just surprised."

"That it's functional? Or that I have a pink hammer?"

"That you'd choose something so frivolous. You told me the day we met that you weren't into frivolous things."

"The hammer isn't frivolous. It's functional and cute. And if you keep making fun of it, you might just end up with one for Christmas."

"We're going to exchange Christmas gifts?" He raised a brow, a smile hovering at the corner of his lips.

"Maybe. If I live that long." She meant it as a joke, but the words fell flat, the worry behind them seeping through. "Forget I said that."

"You know I can't." His hand cupped her jaw, his fingers caressing the tender flesh near her ear. "And you know I'm going to tell you everything will be okay. That Christmas will come and you'll be here to see it."

"I wish I were as confident of that as you are."

"I'll be confident for both of us." His gaze drifted from her eyes to her mouth, his fingers smoothing a trail from her jaw to her neck as he leaned toward her. "I shouldn't do this."

"No, you shouldn't."

"So tell me to stop."

She should, she really should. But she didn't. And as he leaned toward her, she leaned forward. Just a fraction of an inch, but it was enough. His lips brushed hers, the contact shivering through her.

She jerked back, nearly falling into the closet.

"Whoa!" Ben grabbed her arm, pulling her up before she landed in a heap on top of her shoes. "Careful."

"Sorry." Her cheeks were on fire, her heart skipping. This was definitely not good.

So why did she feel so happy about it?

"Don't apologize." Ben seemed completely unperturbed. "I'm not planning to."

He strode out of the room and out the front door, leaving Chloe alone with the two puppies. Curled up on the kitchen floor, neither bothered to rouse as she grabbed aspirin from the counter and swallowed two.

Ben had kissed her.

Or maybe she'd kissed Ben.

She wasn't sure which was more the truth and was pretty sure it didn't matter. After almost a year of saying that she would never, ever, *ever* get involved with another man, she'd just allowed herself to do exactly that.

"This isn't good, boys. It isn't good at all."

Neither of the puppies responded and Chloe dropped down into a chair, wincing as her leg protested the movement. "I think I need to go back to sleep and start this day all over again."

But she couldn't.

So the best thing she could do was get busy, take her mind off her terror and her confusing feelings for Ben.

Confusing?

Not hardly.

She knew exactly what she was feeling. That was the problem.

"Enough of this. I've got plenty to do besides mooning over a man."

She logged onto her computer, pulled up her address book and dialed James Kelly's home number. Adam's business partner and fellow private investigator, James had been the one who'd first contacted Chloe, bringing her in on an investigation he and Adam were working together.

He'd been thrilled when she and Adam began dating, devastated when they'd broken up. In the months following Adam's death, shared grief had made Chloe's friendship with James even stronger.

Still, talking to him about Adam's betrayal, trying to get information about the woman he'd been seeing, wasn't something Chloe had ever planned to do.

"Hello?"

"James? It's Chloe."

"Finally. My wife's been telling me not to call and check in on you, but I was getting close to ignoring her suggestion and giving you a ring."

"Were you really going to call to see how I was doing or were you going to call and ask me to take on a few cases?"

"Maybe a little of both."

Chloe smiled, imagining James's round face and balding head. A year older than his friend, James had always been more settled, more staid, maybe a little more boring than Adam. His generous spirit and calm nature had drawn others to him and had been the backbone of the private investigation service he'd co-owned with Adam. "Then I'll answer both. I'm doing fine. I don't freelance anymore."

"That's too bad. I haven't been able to find anyone as good as you."

"Or as reasonably priced?"

"That, too." There was a smile in his voice and Chloe felt some of the tension of the day easing.

"Keep looking. Eventually you will."

"If you'd agree to do a few simple jobs for me, I wouldn't have to go to all that effort."

"Few and simple? I doubt it."

James chuckled. "True. So, if you didn't call to tell me you were going back to work, what did you call about?"

"I have a favor to ask."

"Go ahead."

"Do you still have Adam's work laptop?"

"In my office. It hasn't been used since…he passed away."

"Do you mind if I take a look at it?"

"Take a look at it as in dig inside and see what you find?"

"Yes."

"Should I ask why?"

"It's complicated."

"I don't like the sound of that. Is everything okay?"

"It'll be better after I get the laptop." She hoped.

"I'll have Jordyn send it to you first thing tomorrow morning. Do we have your new address on file?"

"I gave it to Jordyn before I left."

"Then you can expect to get the laptop by the end of the week. And I'll be expecting to hear just exactly what you were searching for once you find it."

"It's a deal, James. Thanks a lot." She hesitated, not wanting to ask the next question no matter how much she knew it needed asking. "Listen, there's one more thing."

"What's that?"

"I've been wondering about the months before the accident. Adam didn't seem like himself in the weeks before it happened."

"You two had broken up. It was a pretty rough time for him."

"You know why we broke up, right?" She hadn't told him, but she was sure Adam had.

He was silent for a moment, then spoke quietly, his voice more subdued. "Yes. I was surprised and disappointed when Adam told me he was the cause. You two were the perfect match. I told him I couldn't understand why he'd mess that up."

Chloe ignored the last comment, not wanting to discuss her own disappointments, her own sense of failure. "You said you were surprised. You didn't know he was seeing someone?"

"Not until after the breakup. Even then he probably wouldn't have told me. If…"

"What?"

"I was being a little hard on you. I thought you'd just decided to call things off. He didn't want you taking the rap, so he told me what'd happened."

"Did he tell you who the other woman was?"

"No."

"Would you tell me if he had?"

"Chloe, Adam is gone. I don't have to keep his secrets anymore." The sadness in his voice was unmistakable and Chloe could feel her own grief welling up.

"Do you think there's anyone who does know?"

"You know how he was. A different lunch da—companion every day. Too many friends to count. He had more on his social calendar for a week than I usually have all month, but I doubt there was anyone who knew him better than we did. If neither us knew who she was. No one did." He sighed.

"You're right, but if you think of anything—or anyone—"

"I'll let you know." He sighed. "I've got to get going. My wife is waiting for me to take her to dinner. Jordyn will send you the laptop. Let me know if you need anything else. And if you decide to go back to freelancing, I want to be the first client on your list."

"I'll keep that in mind."

"He really did love you, Chloe. You know that don't you?"

"No." She swallowed back sadness and regret. "I don't, but thanks for saying it. I'll be in touch."

She hung up the phone before he could say more, unwilling to discuss what she mostly refused to even think about. Maybe he was right, maybe Adam *had* loved her in his own way. But in the end that hadn't been enough for either of them.

Chloe forced her sadness away, forced herself to brew a pot of coffee, to feed the puppies, to get her mind off the past and into the present. Ben would be back soon. They'd put new locks and bolts on the doors, but Chloe wasn't foolish enough to think that would keep her safe. Only one thing could do that—finding the person stalking her. In a couple days, she'd have both of Adam's computers. If there was information on them, some hint about what had been going on in the months before his death, she'd find it.

NINETEEN

Monday morning came too early, the alarm sounding an insistent beep that pulled Chloe from restless sleep and into the new day. She groaned and yanked the covers over her head, wishing she could ignore the sound and go back to sleep.

Unfortunately, even if she'd been willing to face Opal's wrath—which she wasn't—she couldn't ignore Abel's muffled cries. Obviously he was as ready to be out of his bed as Chloe was to stay in hers.

"I'm coming."

She felt sluggish and off balance as she stumbled to the shower wishing she'd gotten into bed at a much earlier hour. Especially since she'd done absolutely nothing constructive during the hours she'd been awake. After she and Ben put bolts on the front and balcony doors, he'd left for home, rushing to get ready for the evening service. A service Chloe might have attended if she hadn't been worried about what might happen in her apartment during her absence.

And if she hadn't wanted to put some distance between herself and Ben.

Working together in the apartment had felt comfortable, their movements in sync, their conversations easy;

Chloe had found herself thinking about spending time with him next week, next month, next year. That worried her almost as much as the kiss.

So, instead of enjoying fellowship and fun, she'd locked herself in the apartment and spent most of the night pacing the floor, checking the locks, listening for footfalls on the stairs, imagining the doorknob slowly turning.

"Good choice, Chloe." She scowled at her reflection in the mirror as she scraped still-wet hair into a ponytail. Her skin was pallid, the freckles on her nose and cheeks standing out in stark relief, the hollows under her cheeks shadowed. The day had barely begun and she was already tired and out of sorts. The worst part was, she'd left the container of brownies at Ben's house the previous day and couldn't find a drop of chocolate in the house.

"Opal better have some at the shop, Abel, or I'm going to leave you with her and go hunt some down." She lifted the puppy, attached his leash and started toward the front door.

As tired as she felt, she was glad to be going to work. At least when she was at Blooming Baskets she wouldn't be alone. Opal would be there, customers would drop by, Jenna would probably stop in for a few hours with the baby. There'd be plenty to keep Chloe's mind off her nightmares.

And off Ben.

And the kiss.

And the way her heart melted when she looked into his eyes.

"Stop it! He's a man. Just like any other man you know."

Liar.

Maybe. But she wasn't going to admit it. Nor would she spend any more time thinking about a man who seemed too good to be true and probably was.

"Too good to be true is always bad news, right, pup?"

Abel barked his agreement and Chloe stepped out of the apartment and started down the stairs. The house was quiet. The retired couple across the hall were probably still asleep, but downstairs soft music drifted from beneath the door that led to Connor's apartment. For a split second, Chloe considered knocking on his door and asking for an escort to her car, but she had mace in her pocket, a panic button on her key chain. An escort seemed like overkill, though it definitely would have gone a long way in making her want to walk out the door.

Outside, clouds boiled up from the horizon, the steel gray of the sky doing nothing to lift Chloe's mood. The silvery sheen of the lake, the gray-brown bark of the trees, the fall-brown grass, sapped the world of color and life, creating a place of silence. Of death.

"Forget going to Blooming Baskets and *hoping* for chocolate. I'm going to make sure I get some." She muttered the words as she put Abel in the back seat of the car and slammed the door shut.

Twenty minutes later, she strode into Blooming Baskets, a paper bag in one hand, Abel's leash and a drink carrier in the other. Coffee for Opal. Hot chocolate for herself.

Opal stepped out of the back room, a small white basket in her hands and a scowl on her face. "It's about time you got here. I was worried sick wondering what had happened to you."

"I'm not due in for five minutes."

"Chloe Davidson, every day for the past two weeks, you've been here at 7:45. It is now 7:55. You've aged me ten years for every minute. Do you realize how many years that makes me?"

"A hundred and sixty-four?" Chloe tried not to laugh as she set the bag on the front counter.

"Exactly."

"Sorry. I didn't realize you'd be worried."

"Didn't you? Just wait. One day you'll have kids. Then you'll know what it is to wait for someone to call and let you know they're okay."

"I don't think kids are in my future, Opal."

"You'd make a great mother."

"That won't be an issue since I'm not planning on getting married." She passed Opal the cup of coffee, telling herself that what she was saying was absolutely the truth. She was not interested in men. And she was not interested in Ben.

"You brought me coffee?"

"Consider it a peace offering. I really am sorry I worried you, but every once in a while a girl's just got to have chocolate."

"Is that what you've got in the bag?"

"Yep. Two chocolate cake doughnuts. Each."

"Are they glazed?"

"Are there any other kind"

"Not in my mind." Opal smiled, pulled a doughnut out of the bag and handed it to Chloe.

"Eat. You're looking pale again."

"I didn't sleep well last night."

"Probably the puppy keeping you awake."

"Probably. What's on the schedule for today?"

"Plenty. Four baskets for the missionary luncheon at Grace Christian. Prep for the Costello wedding shower this Saturday. Two arrangements for the hospital. One that needs to be delivered to a retirement village outside of town. Two to private residents."

"Are you delivering or am I?"

"I am. It'll take me less time."

"Because you're a lead foot."

"Because I know where I'm going. Besides, you do look exhausted. It's probably for the best that you not spend the day driving around. And I think we'll skip tonight, too. I can't drag you out shopping when you're so exhausted."

"You weren't going to be dragging me, Opal. I was happy to go with you."

"Be that as it may, you're not going to go. Betsy Reynolds has decided to go to Richmond, too. She called me last night and was begging me to go shopping with her. I'll just call and tell her I can do it after all."

"So I'm being replaced," Chloe teased, biting into the rich chocolate doughnut, happy to be out of the apartment and away from her worries for a while. She had made plenty of mistakes in her life, but coming to Lakeview wasn't one of them. Maybe she hadn't quite gotten the hang of floral design, but at least she had some measure of stability in her life again. She also had Opal and that was worth its weight in gold.

"Not yet, but if you keep talking instead of working, I just might have to." Opal's amused words were enough to get Chloe moving, and she lifted Abel and brought him to the back room.

It didn't take long to ease into the flow of the day. By noon, Opal was out in the van making her deliveries and Chloe was cleaning up petals and stems from the work area in the back of the shop. She tried to work quickly, but the sluggish feeling she'd woken with hadn't left despite hot chocolate, two cups of coffee and a sugar-laden doughnut.

Doughnuts. She'd managed to eat both of hers.

The bell over the front door rang and she stepped out into the front of the shop, pasting a smile on her face and hoping she looked more lively than she felt.

"Hi, can I help…?" The question died on her lips as she caught sight of Ben, his jaw shadowed by a beard, his eyes blazing brilliant blue, a smile curving his lips. Dark jeans. A soft flannel shirt layered over a black T-shirt that hugged well-defined muscles. He looked good, really good.

Chloe resisted the urge to smooth the strands of hair that had fallen from her ponytail and were straggling around her face. "Ben, what are you doing here?"

"I was driving by and thought I'd stop in to see how you were doing."

"Driving by?"

"Driving by on my way here to see how you're doing."

Laughter bubbled up and spilled out, filling the room and chasing away the anxiety that had plagued Chloe all morning. "Thanks."

"For what?" He stepped closer, reaching for her hand and tugging her out from behind the display case, his gaze taking in her black pants and pink shirt, her scraggly hair and makeup-free face.

"For stopping in to see how I was doing. And for making me laugh."

"You're welcome." He did what she hadn't, reaching out and smoothing strands of hair from her cheeks, his fingers blazing trails of warmth that made her heart race.

She stepped back, her face heating, her mind shouting that if she didn't watch it she'd be in big trouble. That she was already *in* big trouble.

"So how *are* you doing?"

"I'm doing great."

"Liar."

"I'm doing okay."

"Try again."

"I feel lousy. Happy now?"

"Not even close." He ran a hand over his jaw. "I won't be happy until we find the person who's after you."

"*If* we find the person." *Before he finishes what he started.* She didn't say the rest, but it was what she'd been thinking during the darkest hours of the night and what she was still thinking in the cold gray light of the November day.

"We'll find him. Jake's heading in the right direction with the investigation. I feel strongly about that. So does he."

"You spoke to him today?"

"I stopped by his office before I came here."

"I wish you hadn't."

"Because you think I'm getting too involved?" He crossed his arms over his chest, his stance relaxed, but alert, his gaze just a little hard.

"Because I don't want you involved at all." At least her head didn't. Her heart was another matter entirely.

"Funny, I don't think that's the truth, either."

"The truth is simple. Getting involved with me is dangerous. Anyone in his right mind would see that and go running in the other direction." Chloe shoved her bangs out of her eyes, grabbed a small white basket from behind the counter, then stalked across the room to pull white and pink roses from the cooler.

"I'm not just anyone. And I'm not running." The hint of steel in his voice surprised Chloe and she met his eyes, saw the hard determination there.

"Ben—"

"Maybe you're used to people abandoning you when things get tough, but that's not my style. Whatever happens in the next days, weeks or months, I plan to be part of it."

"Why? We've known each other a week—"

"Ten days." He grinned, but the steel was still there.

"My point is, you don't have a commitment to me. There's no reason for you to get more involved in my problems then you already are."

"Whether or not I have a commitment to you has nothing to do with it."

"It has everything to do with it." She placed a square of floral foam in the bottom of the basket and jabbed a rose into it. "We barely know each other and you're letting yourself get caught up in my mess. You could be off doing a hundred other things that would be a lot less dangerous to your health."

"And yet here I am." He grabbed her hand before she could mash another rose into the arrangement. "Don't you think there's a reason for that, Chloe? A reason God brought us into each other's lives at exactly this time?"

"I stopped thinking I understood God's ways months ago." She slid her hand away from his, using less force to place the next flower.

"You don't have to understand, you just have to trust."

She looked up and into the vibrant blue depths of his eyes, felt herself drawn into them and into his certainty. "Trust isn't easy for me."

"It's not easy for anyone when things get tough. We doubt. We question. In the end, we either choose to believe God is still working His will through our lives or we end up turning away from our faith. I don't think you're the kind to turn away."

"You're right. I'm not." But there had been times before she'd come to Lakeview that she'd wondered if she might, if maybe everything she'd believed, everything she'd trusted in was a lie.

She pulled baby's breath from the cooler, shoving a few stems in between the roses.

"Then have faith that God put me into your life for a reason and stop worrying so much about what that might mean." Ben pulled baby's breath from the pile she'd set on the counter and pressed the stem into the foam, his knuckles brushing against hers, the simple act of working together sealing the connection that shouldn't be between them, but was.

"You're wrong, Ben. I do have to worry about what that might mean."

"Because you're afraid of what might happen to anyone who gets close to you?"

"Because I've *lived* what might happen to anyone who gets close to me and I don't want to live it again."

"You're not going to."

"You can't know that."

"No, I can't." His knuckles brushed against hers again, but this time he turned his hand and captured her fingers, his thumb caressing the tender flesh on the underside of her wrist. "But I do know this—there's nothing in the world that can keep God's will and plan from being worked out and His plan is always for our best. Whatever happens, it'll be okay."

He tugged her forward so that she was leaning over the glass display case, just inches from Ben and the strength he offered. For a moment she was sure he would kiss her again. She thought about moving forward, thought about pulling back, hadn't quite decided between the two when he brushed a hand over her hair.

A pink petal fluttered down and settled in the floral arrangement she was designing.

"Were you fighting with roses when I got here?"

"I was fighting with Abel who was fighting with pink hydrangea. Opal will not be pleased."

"I bet not. Will she be back soon?"

"Probably within the hour."

"And you're here alone until then?"

"Yes."

"I'm not sure that's such a good idea."

"Good idea or not, it is what it is." Chloe shoved more baby's breath into the sea of white and pink roses and frowned. "This isn't exactly going the way I planned."

"What'd you plan?"

"Something that looked a lot better."

He eyed the floral arrangement and Chloe expected him to say what most people would—it looks great. Instead, he pulled a few roses from the middle of the basket, spaced them closer to the edge of the foam. "Maybe a little more of the filler would help."

"A pastor, a chef *and* a floral designer. Is there anything you can't do?"

"I can't leave you alone here by yourself."

"Sure you can. Just walk out the door."

"Not until Opal gets here. So, what do you say we finish this and order a pizza? I don't know about you, but I'm ready for lunch."

"Ben—"

"It's just lunch."

"It's just you babysitting me."

"It doesn't feel anything at all like babysitting to me." The words were warm and filled with promise.

"I don't think this is a good idea."

"Good idea or not, it is what it is." He smiled, his eyes flashing with amusement.

And suddenly having him around didn't seem like such a bad thing. Despite her worry, despite her fear, for just a while, Chloe decided to believe what Ben had said—that God had put him in her life for a reason, that a divine plan was being worked out and that in the end everything would be okay.

TWENTY

There were two messages on Chloe's machine when she got home. The first from Karen telling her that Adam's hard drive was on the way. The second was from Adam's former receptionist, Jordyn Winslow. She'd mailed the laptop and wanted to know if Chloe needed anything else.

Chloe glanced at the clock as she stripped off her jacket. Jordyn had her ear to the ground when it came to matters that involved anything to do with Adam and James's business or their personal lives. She prided herself on knowing their schedules during work and away from it. If there was anyone besides James who might have an idea of who Adam had been seeing, it was Jordyn.

It was just past five when Chloe picked up the phone, almost hoping that the receptionist had left for the day. It would be much easier to leave a message than to ask what needed asking in person.

Her hopes were dashed when Jordyn's chipper voice filled the line.

"Kelly and Hill Investigative Services. Can I help you?" The greeting was the same, but different. Adam's name no longer a part of it. Grief speared Chloe's heart, making her mute for a moment too long.

"*Hello?* Can I help you?" Jordyn's tone had lost some of its peppiness.

"Jordyn, it's Chloe."

"Hi, Chloe. It's good to hear from you. James said you're settling in down there. Is it as peaceful as you were hoping?"

"Yes. The lake is beautiful and the area is much quieter than D.C."

"I bet. Personally, I'm not sure I could do what you've done. Move out to the country. Too many years of suburban life have spoiled me. I like the convenience of having everything close by. I don't know how you're keeping your sanity." Was the comment about sanity a subtle jab? Chloe could never be sure with Jordyn. They'd known each other for the three years Chloe had been freelancing for the company, but they'd never been friends.

"Rural life isn't for everyone, but it's definitely for me."

"To each her own, I suppose. Though I'm not sure what the point of giving up a lucrative business to become a florist was. You'd done well for yourself, Chloe. It's a shame to waste all those years of work." Jordyn's words were patronizing, but Chloe didn't let them bother her. A fixture at Adam and James's office since they'd partnered as private investigators ten years before, Jordyn had an opinion about most things and wasn't afraid to share them.

"Like you said, to each her own. My decision might not make sense to you, but I haven't regretted it." Chloe set fresh water and food down for Abel and limped to the balcony, unbolting the French doors and stepping out in the crisp evening air.

"Yes, well, we'll see how you feel in a month. Did you get my message?"

"Yes, thanks for sending the laptop out."

"James said you needed it ASAP. I wasn't sure there was quite as much hurry as he made it out to be, but humored him anyway. You know how men can be."

Not really, but she didn't plan to admit that to Jordyn whose blond-haired beauty attracted more men than Chloe had ever been able to keep track of. "They're interesting, that's for sure."

"*Interesting?* Frustrating is more the word I was thinking. Anyway, the laptop is on the way. You should receive it by the end of the week. James didn't say what you needed it for."

Chloe decided the nonquestion needed no response, and she ignored it. "I appreciate you getting it out so quickly, Jordyn. I know how busy you are."

"Not as busy anymore. Adam kept things hopping around here. Without him, things just aren't the same."

"Adam did love his job." *Go ahead, bring it up. Ask her before you chicken out.* "Jordyn, you asked if I needed anything else, and I was wondering…"

If she knew who Adam had cheated with? If she'd watched him leave for lunch with his girlfriend and silently applauded Chloe's downfall.

"What?"

"Adam was seeing someone besides me. I wondered if you knew who it was." There, it was out, and a lot less painful to say than she'd thought it would be.

"I'd heard rumors that's why the two of you broke up, but I didn't want to believe it was true. Adam seemed like such a loyal type of guy."

"Yeah, he did. I guess you don't know who he was seeing?"

"I'm afraid not."

"All right. Thanks anyway."

"No problem. Do me a favor and call me when the laptop arrives, okay? I've got it insured and want to make sure it gets there in one piece."

"Sure."

"Great. I'll talk to you soon, then." The phone line went dead, and Chloe set the receiver down. James didn't know who Adam had been seeing. Jordyn didn't. Chloe certainly didn't.

But the computers might. One e-mail, that's all it would take. One note that spoke of more than friendship. Deleted or not, they'd be there, buried in the computer, waiting to be found.

Chloe just wasn't sure she was ready to find the information. A nameless, faceless woman was much easier to deal with than a real identity. A name. Maybe a face. Maybe the knowledge that it was someone Chloe knew, had maybe even liked.

Not that it mattered now. Adam was gone, his betrayal minuscule in comparison to his death. All they'd shared—laughter, joy, tears and pain—fading to bittersweet memory.

Hot tears filled Chloe's eyes and she blinked them back, rubbing at the band of scars on her hand, the cool air from the still-opened French doors bathing her heated face. She wanted so badly to go back to the night of the accident, rewind the clock, change the outcome. But the past couldn't be changed. All she could do was move forward into the unknown.

As if he sensed her distress, Abel whined, rolling over on his back and begging for attention. She knelt down and scratched him under the chin. "You're a good puppy. Even if you did destroy the hydrangea and chew the leg of Opal's desk."

His tail thumped the floor, his tongue lolled out, the sight comical and cute. If she'd had her cameras she'd have taken a picture, but Jake hadn't returned them and had made no mention of how long they'd be in his custody. Instead, she straightened, limping into the kitchen and eyeing the contents of her refrigerator. There wasn't much. Some fruit. A bag of baby carrots. A nearly empty half-gallon of milk. Apple juice. Why hadn't she stopped at the store on the way home and picked up groceries?

She dug into the cupboard, found a box of Pop-Tarts, and ripped open the wrapper. They weren't chocolate, but they were better than nothing.

Abel barked, tumbling toward the door, just as a soft rap sounded against the wood.

"Who is it?"

"It's Mrs. Anderson, dear. I've got a package for you."

"A package?" Chloe pulled open the door and smiled at her neighbor, a spry woman of eighty-nine who spent her days volunteering at the community center and her evenings enjoying the company of her husband of sixty years.

"Yes. Charles said it was on the front porch when he came home. I guess it couldn't fit in your mailbox." She held out what looked like a wrapped shoe box. "He thought it best to bring it inside. No sense leaving it outside for thieves to get."

"Thank you for bringing it over, Mrs. Anderson. And please tell your husband I appreciate him bringing it inside."

"It was no problem at all, dear. Now, I've got to run. It's senior night at the movie theater and Charles and I are going to meet some friends there."

"Have fun."

"You, too."

Chloe waited until the elderly woman was back inside her apartment, then closed the door and bolted it. The package was light and wrapped in brown packing paper, her name and address printed in broad, firm letters on one side. She turned the package over, saw no sign of a return address, nothing to indicate where it had come from.

A warning shivered along her spine, the box like a coiled serpent ready to strike. Anything could be inside. Pictures. Letters. Poison. Body parts.

"Okay. You're really losing it, Chloe. Knock it off before you convince yourself there are explosives inside and call the bomb squad to rescue you."

She set the box on the kitchen table, took a steak knife and slit through tape and paper. There was more paper beneath, bright yellow wrapping paper that she made quick work of. The white box inside looked innocuous enough, but there was no card or note. There also weren't any blood stains or awful odors, but that didn't mean there wasn't something awful inside.

Finally, Chloe couldn't put off the inevitable any longer. She braced herself and lifted the lid, nearly laughing out loud when she saw what was inside. A brown and green turtle was shoved into the small space, one golden eye staring up at her.

She pulled it out, smiling as she saw the dog tag hanging from a string around its neck. Speedy Too.

Ben.

How he'd managed to find a floppy stuffed turtle, Chloe didn't know. Why he'd taken the time to buy it and send it to her was something she wasn't sure she *wanted* to know.

Everything else aside—all the danger, all the fear, all the nightmares—she wasn't ready to get involved in a relationship. She wasn't sure she'd ever be ready for that.

But if she were, someone like Ben would be perfect….

Don't even go there, Chloe. Don't even think about it. Ben is a charming guy with a congregation of single women standing in line hoping to get his attention. Let them. You're not interested.

Aren't you?

She ran her hand over the turtle's shell, imagining Ben buying it and the dog tag, wrapping them in the box, going to the post office. He'd gone through a lot of trouble and that wasn't something many people had done for her in the past.

She grabbed the phone, found Ben's number and dialed.

"Hello?" His voice rumbled across the line, comfortably familiar and much too welcome.

"Hi, Ben. It's Chloe."

"Hey. Everything okay?" His voice deepened, warmed, pulled her in.

"Fine." She smoothed her hand over the turtle again, her throat tight for reasons she refused to name. "I got a package in the mail today."

"Did you?"

"No return address. No note. At first I thought it might be an unpleasant surprise."

"More mutilated pictures?"

"I was thinking something explosive. I got pretty close to calling the bomb squad."

"That would have made interesting news for the gossip mill."

"Fortunately, it didn't come to that."

"No?"

"It seems someone has a thing for turtles. Speedy ones."

"You don't say."

"I do. And I also say that that someone shouldn't have gone to so much trouble."

"Who said it was any trouble? Maybe that someone happened to be shopping for a birthday present for his niece and saw the turtle and thought of you."

"And just happened to find a pet tag with the perfect name written on it?"

"Something like that." He laughed, the sound rumbling across the phone line.

"You could have just brought it over. It would have saved you the effort and the cost of postage."

"And have you give me a hundred reasons why you couldn't accept it?"

"I wouldn't have given you a hundred reasons."

"Sure you would have. And then I would have felt obligated to list a hundred reasons why you *could* accept it. That seemed like a lot more effort than putting it in the box and mailing it."

Chloe smiled, setting Speedy Too down on the counter and crossing to the balcony. The night was clear, the stars bright in the indigo sky. "You're probably right. I would have argued, but in the end you would have convinced me. Speedy Too is the most thoughtful gift I've ever received."

"Then I'm glad I followed my gut and bought it."

"Ben, I'm not sure what you want from me, but—"

"I don't want anything from you, but friendship."

"A kiss is a little more than friendship."

"Let's chalk that up to a momentary lapse of judgment and forget it happened."

"I don't think that's possible."

"And *I* think I'm flattered."

Chloe's cheeks heated, and she was glad Ben wasn't there to see it. "You know what I mean. A kiss changes everything. It takes nothing and makes it into something."

"What's between us could never be nothing. Kiss or no kiss."

"That's just the thing. I don't want there to be something between us."

"There already is." He sighed, and she could picture him standing in his kitchen, maybe a cup of coffee in his hands, his hair falling across his forehead.

"I—"

"Let's be friends for a while, Chloe. We can worry about what comes next later."

"Nothing is going to come next."

"You just keep telling yourself that."

"I will. And now I've really got to go. Abel needs some attention."

Chloe could hear Ben's laughter as she hung up the phone and she couldn't stop her answering smile. He was right. There was something between them. From the moment she'd met him she'd felt the connection, a living thing that seemed to be growing with every moment they spent together.

Friendship.

She liked the sound of that.

The silence of the night wrapped around her, the bright stars and crescent moon hanging over the dark lake, the distant mountains rising up to touch the sky. God's creation. His design. Ready for His purpose. His will. Whatever that might be.

Maybe one day Chloe would know. For now, she could

barely see the beauty for the shadows. She shuddered, stepping back into the apartment and closing the door against the darkness.

Abel tumbled near her feet as she sat down in front of her laptop and pulled up work files. Maybe she'd missed something in her previous searches. Maybe there was something there still waiting to be discovered.

She could only pray that if there was, she'd find it soon because no matter how confident Ben and Jake were, Chloe had a feeling that all her fears were about to come true and that the nightmare she'd been running from for months would soon overtake her.

TWENTY-ONE

Three nights and eighteen hours of searching computer files revealed no secrets that seemed worth killing to keep hidden. Jake's investigation seemed to be turning up just as few leads. When he stopped by the shop Thursday to tell her there'd been no fingerprints on the frame or photo and that a man they'd identified as the owner of the PO box had gone to ground and couldn't be located, Chloe was ready to lock up the shop and go home.

If it hadn't been just a little past nine in the morning, she might have.

The day seemed to stretch on for an eternity, and by the time she was ready to close Blooming Baskets for the evening, Chloe wanted nothing more than a hot bath to sooth her aching leg and a warm bed to hide in. That's exactly what she planned to have. *After* she did the exercises the orthopedic specialist had recommended during Chloe's appointment the previous day and *after* she fed Opal's demon cat and checked her mail.

Unfortunately, doing the last meant making the fifteen-minute drive to Opal's house in the dark, getting out of the Mustang in the dark, walking into a dark house in the dark.

"I've got to stop this kind of negative thinking, Abel.

Dark, dark, dark, dark. Obsessing on it is only making me more nervous. I need to refocus my thoughts. Try to look at the bright side of things." Chloe stopped at the head of Opal's driveway, reaching out her window to pull mail out of the box, then following the winding path toward the ranch-style house her friend owned. Built in the seventies, the house wasn't nearly as fancy as some of its neighbors, but the three-acre lakefront lot was a premium and Opal loved it.

Chloe loved it, too. Her fondest childhood memories centered around Opal and her family, their house, the lake and the small cottage next door where Chloe had spent seven summers of her life.

She pulled up in front of the house and turned off the engine, the headlights dying and leaving the area shadowed and foreboding.

As fond as her memories of the place were, Chloe wasn't sure she wanted to get out of the car and go into the house. It looked different at night, the windows gaping wounds that bled darkness, the front door an ebony slash against the pale siding. Abandoned. Lonely. The kind of place where bad things might happen and probably would.

"But it's just a house, right? There's no one lurking in the shadows, waiting for me to get out of the car."

Abel snored in response, his head resting on his paws as he snoozed on the back seat. "You know you're supposed to be a companion, a watchdog, a fierce defender of your human, don't you?"

Abel opened one eye and closed it again.

"Obviously, I'm on my own on this one. Which is okay, because I can handle it." She took a deep breath, pulled Opal's keys from her purse and started to open the car door. Headlights shone in the rearview mirror, the unexpected brightness nearly blinding Chloe. She jumped, jamming her car keys back into the ignition, fear squeezing the breath from her lungs. No one should be coming down the driveway while Opal was away. She needed to put the car in reverse and drive away while she still could, but the oncoming car blocked her retreat, the blue spruce that lined the driveway prevented her from pulling around it.

She was trapped.

No. Not trapped. All she had to do was use her cell phone and call for help. Of course, by the time help arrived it might be too late. She'd be lying dead on the pavement.

Get out of the car. Go in the house. Call for help.

She grabbed her purse, Opal's keys still in her hand, and jumped from the car, racing toward the house, headlights pinning her against the gray-black night.

An easy target to see.

An easy one to take out with a gun.

Or to ram with a car.

There were a million ways Chloe could be killed here in the dark in front of Opal's house, but not if she could get inside the house first.

A door slammed, someone shouted, but Chloe's focus was on the door and safety. She shoved the keys into the lock, opened the door, jerked it closed again.

The doorbell rang before she could even turn the lock, the sound so jarring Chloe stumbled forward, knocking into the door, her cell phone tumbling from her hand. She landed hard on her knees, her pulse echoing hollowly in her ears as the doorbell chimed again and the door swung open.

A dark figure loomed in the threshold, then crouched beside her, the scent of pine and man enveloping Chloe as he leaned close. "You run pretty fast for a woman with one bad leg."

Ben.

She didn't know whether to hug him or hit him and settled for accepting the hand he offered and allowing herself to be pulled to her feet. "I wasn't expecting company."

"Neither was I. Are you okay?"

"Besides my wounded pride, I'm fine. I need to go out and get Abel, though. He might not be doing as well out alone in a strange place."

"He's fine. I grabbed him and put him back in your car before he could get too far."

"Thanks. Should I ask why you're here?"

"Opal called me this morning and asked me to stop by to feed her cat. Apparently he likes to be fed at six o'clock on the dot."

"Not a minute sooner."

"Or later."

"It sounds like she told you the exact same thing she told me."

"That her cat is finicky and refuses to eat if the food is put in his bowl at any other time of the day and that when Opal's daughter took care of Checkers he didn't eat the entire time, because she fed him in the morning."

"Verbatim." Chloe raked a hand through her hair and shook her head. Amused. Irritated. Happy that Ben was there with her, but not sure she was happy to be feeling that way.

"You know she's matchmaking, right?" Ben flicked on the light, spreading a warm glow through the small living room and illuminating his tan face and sandy hair, his vivid eyes, the hard angle of his jaw and the soft curve of his lips.

"Yeah, and I cannot believe that the same woman who

told her kids to keep their noses out of other people's business is sticking hers into ours."

"She probably figured she was killing two birds with one stone. She gets us together for a few minutes and makes sure you're safe."

"You're probably right. What happened Sunday really shook her. I think she was hoping I'd be safer here than I'd been in D.C."

"You will be soon."

"I hope you're right, but to be honest, I'm not so sure. I've been researching my old case files for the past three nights and I can't find anything even remotely suspicious."

"Have you heard from Jake?"

"Yeah, he's coming up empty, too. The biggest lead he has is the PO box, but the owner has disappeared."

"How about the phone records?"

"Jake hasn't mentioned them, probably for fear of embarrassing me. No doubt there were thousands of calls, most of them from women."

"That's Adam's embarrassment, not yours."

"Is it? Because it doesn't feel that way." She moved through the house, not wanting to continue the conversation.

The living room opened into a modern kitchen, the white cupboards, tile floor and granite counters much different than the dark wood and linoleum of past years. Despite the changes, the room had the same homey feel as it had when Chloe was a girl, the taupe walls, white wainscoting, and deep blue chair rail inviting all who visited to stay awhile.

Checkers, however, wasn't as welcoming.

He stood in one corner of the room, guarding two porcelain bowls, his tubby black-and-white body stiff with irritation.

"All right, cat. We can do this the hard way, or the easy way."

"I take it you've had run-ins with him before?" Ben moved into the kitchen, his hand wrapping around her arm as he moved between her and the cat.

"Yes. At our very first meeting. The one and only time I've been here since I've been back in Lakeview."

"Bite or scratch?"

"Scratch."

"Then he doesn't completely despise you. Last time I was here, he nearly chewed through my thumb."

"Then I guess you'd better keep your distance. Your congregation won't be happy with me if you show up Sunday with a digit missing."

"Are you kidding me? I consider this a personal challenge. Do you know where Opal keeps the cat food?"

"In the cupboard under the sink."

"Okay. So, here's the plan. I'll distract him. You grab the food and pour it into the bowl."

Chloe pulled a plastic container filled with cat food out from under the cupboard and turned toward Checkers.

He hissed, his tail fluffing, his golden eyes glittering.

"Is there a plan B?"

"I'm afraid not." Ben smiled and grabbed a dish towel that hung from the refrigerator door handle. "Ready?"

"As I'll ever be."

He stepped forward, trailing the towel on the floor in front of the cat. "Come on, kitty, out of the way."

Checkers leaped past him, yowling wildly as he raced from the room.

"I thought maybe he'd play, but I guess scare tactics work just as well."

"He'll be back." Chloe poured the food and refilled the water dish. "But our mission is accomplished."

"With no casualties." Ben took the food container from her hand and returned it. "We make a good team."

They did. That was the problem. They seemed to complement each other almost too much, fitting into each other's lives with almost frightening ease, as if they'd known each other years rather than days. If the circumstances had been different, if *Chloe* were different, her heart would probably flutter with anticipation every time she saw him, her mind jumping forward weeks and months and imagining the relationship lasting far into the future.

Who was she kidding? Her mind already did.

"Hey." His hands framed her face, forcing her to look up and into his eyes before they smoothed back into the loose strands of her hair. "Whatever you're worrying about, don't."

"I'm not worrying." She spoke lightly and leaned away from his touch, but he didn't release his hold, his hands dropping to her shoulders, his thumbs caressing the skin over her collarbones.

"You *are* worrying. Maybe about the case. Maybe about us."

Us. He spoke the word with confidence. As if they weren't just a team, but a couple. "Ben—"

"But you don't need to worry, Chloe. Between you, me and Jake, we'll find the person who's after you." He paused. "As for us, we're friends. There's nothing to worry about there."

Friends? He'd claimed that twice now and she hadn't believed him either time. As much as she didn't want it, the truth was in her mind, in her heart. What was between them now might be friendship, but it was something more, too. "You keep saying we're friends, Ben, but I get the feeling you might be interested in something more."

His eyes blazed into hers. Then, as if he'd banked whatever fire was inside, they cooled. "What I'm interested in is entirely up to you. Come on, we need to finish up here. I've got a business meeting at the church in half an hour. And you need to get home and rest up for tomorrow night when we tackle the Reed kids together."

The end to the conversation was purposeful and Chloe didn't see any reason to try to continue it. What would she say? What could she say? If things were up to her, she'd...

What?

Be content with friendship?

Try for something more?

She didn't know. Couldn't know until after all the other problems in her life were solved. If they were ever solved. And right now, she wasn't sure they would be.

TWENTY-TWO

Friday night came much more quickly than Chloe was happy with. It wasn't that she didn't want to babysit for Tiffany and Jake's kids, it was simply that she hadn't done any babysitting in years. The closest she'd been to a child under five was at church, and even then she hadn't been hands-on, preferring to stay away from nursery duty in favor of working with teens.

The tiny infant Tiffany placed in her arms was nothing like the teenagers Chloe had worked with. As a matter of fact, he looked way too delicate for her peace of mind. She glanced at the clock over the Reeds' fireplace mantel. Six-oh-five.

Ben had better hurry up. There was no way she wanted to be left alone with two kids under the age of three.

"Did Ben say how long he'd be?" Jake's voice was gruff.

"Actually, he promised to be here before you left. I'm sure he'll be here soon." She hoped. He'd left as soon as they'd finished feeding Checkers, handing her scribbled directions to Jake's house and telling Chloe there was an emergency he had to deal with before meeting her there.

That was forty minutes ago.

Not that she was counting.

"Maybe we should stick around until he gets here." Tiffany touched her son's downy cheek, smiling a little as the baby turned toward her hand.

"We've got reservations, hon. If we're late, we might not get a table."

"Then we'll make new reservations for another night."

"Not on your birthday." He met Chloe's eyes. "Will it be a problem if we leave?"

"No, go ahead. I wouldn't want you to lose your table."

"Isaac's already been fed. Just lay him down in his bassinet and he should drop right off to sleep." Tiffany smoothed a hand over her son's dark hair, the softness in her face, the love in her eyes so obvious it almost hurt to look at.

Chloe glanced down at the baby's smooth skin and deep blue eyes. He looked like his father. The little redheaded girl standing close to Jake, a pint-size version of her mother. "Will I need to feed him again before you get back?"

"Nope. We should be home before his next feeding. Right, honey?"

"Three hours tops." Jake speared Chloe with a look that left no doubt about what he was thinking. "You have done this before haven't you?"

"I used to babysit all the time."

"Infants?"

"Yes."

"Toddlers?"

"Yes."

"Then you know how quickly a kid Honor's age can get into trouble."

"I do." She just hoped she was still up to the task of keeping them out of it.

"She needs to be watched at all times. Don't—"

"Honey." Tiffany placed a hand on Jake's arms. "You just said you didn't want to be late. Shouldn't we be going?"

"Right. We won't be far. Just at the clubhouse. If anything happens call me on my cell."

"I will."

Tiffany leaned down to kiss her daughter. "Be good for Ms. Chloe." She straightened and turned back to Chloe. "She can stay up for another half hour. Then she needs to get in bed. Though she might not be as easy to get settled as Isaac."

"I'll do my best. I'm sure everything will be fine."

"It better be." Jake grumbled the words as he leaned over to kiss his daughter, waiting until his wife opened the front door and stepped outside before he speared Chloe with a dark look. "An off-duty friend of mine is going to be here in five minutes. He'll be doing stakeout until Ben shows up. If anything happens, just flick the lights. He'll come in and help until we get back."

"That isn't—" The hard look in his eyes kept her from finishing the thought. "Okay. Great. Have fun."

"You, too." He stepped outside and shut the door, leaving Chloe with a sleepy infant, a bouncy toddler and absolutely no idea what she was going to do with either.

Ben's cell phone rang as he pulled up in front of Jake's house. Forty minutes late. He grimaced, grabbing the phone as he stepped out of the car. "Ben Avery."

"You done with that emergency, yet?" Jake's voice was gritty and soft. Obviously, he'd snuck away from his wife to make the call.

"I just pulled up in front of your house."

"Martin's still there?"

Ben glanced at the small blue pickup parked on the street in front of the house and waved at the off-duty deputy. "Yeah. He's here."

"Good. Do me a favor and tell him he's free to go home, but if he mentions a word of this to my wife, he's fired."

Ben laughed, striding toward the vehicle. "You didn't tell her?"

"And have her lecture me all night about my lack of faith in humankind? I don't think so."

"She's right. You don't have much faith in people."

"Sure I do. It just depends on the people." He paused. "I've got to get back to the table before Tiffany catches on to what I'm doing. Take care of my kids."

"You know I will."

"See you."

Ben sent Martin home and strode toward the restored Queen Ann that Jake and Tiffany lived in. Hopefully, Chloe hadn't had it too hard while he was MIA.

He knocked on the door, bracing himself for utter chaos.

"Who's there?" Chloe's voice sounded through the door, muted, but firm and calm. Maybe things inside the house weren't quite as bad as he'd expected.

"Ben."

"And I should let you in why?"

"Because you can't manage without me?"

"Try again."

"Because I realize the error of my ways and want to apologize?"

"Still not working."

"Because I've got half a dozen chocolate chip cookies in my hand?"

"That'll work." She swung the door open, stepping back

to let him in. The brightly lit foyer with its colorful quilts hanging from the hall was as familiar as Ben's own home.

Chloe was familiar, too. Like an old friend he'd reconnected with rather than someone he'd only recently met. Tonight, she'd left her black hair hanging loose, the bangs falling into her eyes and hiding her expression as they so often did.

"You said you had cookies?"

"Right here." He handed her the bag that Ella had packed for him, smiling when Chloe dug in, pulling out a cookie and biting into it.

"Delicious. So good I think I'll have another." She pulled a second from the bag. "You weren't baking cookies while I was babysitting, were you?"

"I don't think that would get me too many points with you or the Reeds." He shrugged out of his jacket, dropped it onto the couch. "I had a big problem to deal with. It took a little longer than I expected."

"A *little* longer? You said you'd be here before Jake and Tiffany left."

"I tried, but I got held up."

"Is everything okay?"

"I'm happy to report that Mammoth is doing fine."

"Mammoth?" Chloe moved through the foyer and into the kitchen. Ben followed, noting the subtle hitch to her stride and the gingerly way she moved as she bent to pick a stuffed bear from the floor. "Should I ask?"

"He's a pig. His owner lives a few miles outside of town. She collects animals that no one else wants."

"And Mammoth is one of them?"

"Yes. And he lives up to his name. He's huge. When he gets out of his pen, he isn't always easy to corral again."

"Did you manage it?"

"Yeah, but my clothes didn't survive to tell the story. I had to go home and change. How about you? It looks like you managed to settle the troops."

"Nearly. Honor isn't quite asleep yet."

"Maybe I should go peek in on her."

"I don't think you're going to have to." Chloe cocked her head and smiled. "I think I hear the pitter-patter of little feet."

Seconds later, Honor appeared, her chubby cheeks rosy, her smile wide as she raced toward him.

He swooped down to grab her, tickling her belly as he lifted her into his arms. "Hey, little bit, aren't you supposed to be in bed?"

She giggled and wriggled in his arms as he started back toward the hall and the stairs that led to her room. "Want to come?"

Chloe shook her head, a half smile softening her face as she watched. "I think I'll let you settle her down this time."

It didn't take long to tuck Honor back in bed. Convincing her to stay there took a few more minutes. By the time Ben made it back downstairs, Chloe was seated in a chair, a cup of coffee in her hand. "Want some?"

"I think I will. And a couple of those cookies if you saved me any."

"I might have. Sit down. I'll get you the bag and some coffee." She started to rise, but Ben pressed her back down into her seat, not liking the pale cast to her skin or the dark circles beneath her eyes. "I'll get it."

He'd been hoping there'd be swift resolution to Chloe's troubles, that Jake's investigation would quickly lead to a suspect and an arrest. Unfortunately, evidence was elusive, the leads going nowhere.

He had a feeling that the answers they needed were right at their fingertips. More precisely, at Chloe's fingertips. Her investigative skills would lead them to the person they were seeking. It was just a matter of time.

"You're quiet."

Chloe's words pulled him from his thoughts and he carried his coffee and the cookies to the table, taking a seat opposite her. "Just thinking."

"About?"

"You."

Her cheeks heated, the subtle color making her eyes seem even more green, her skin even more silky. "I'm not sure that's a good idea."

"I'm not sure there's anything either of us can do about it." Whether Chloe liked it or not, they'd been brought together for a reason and Ben had every intention of seeing things through to the end. No matter what that might be. "Have you received the laptop and hard drive you were waiting for?"

"Not yet. I'm hoping they'll both be there when I get home. I'm anxious to get started. I think if there are any clues to what's going on, they'll be on one of Adam's computers."

"I was thinking the same."

"If we're right, the case could be solved in days. If we're wrong…" She fiddled with her coffee cup, her long fingers and sturdy hands more capable looking than graceful.

"What?"

"I don't know. That's the scary part. What will happen if we're wrong and I don't find something? What direction can we go except back where we were? Jackson and The Strangers or me going insane."

"The second isn't even a possibility. The first is doubtful."

"And everything else is a mystery?"

"For now, but hopefully not for much longer."

"Hopefully not." She stood and stretched, her slim figure encased in her work uniform of black slacks and a fitted pink sweater, her hair a dark waterfall that slid across her cheek as she leaned over the sink and rinsed her coffee cup.

Ben imagined her doing that in the morning, bright sunlight reflecting off her blue-black hair, her eyes still dark from sleep.

And decided it might be best to force his mind in another direction. "Were the kiddos good for you?"

"Isaac's been asleep the whole time. Honor is a little firecracker, but we had fun."

"You like kids?"

"I guess I do." She leaned against the counter. "I hadn't thought about it much before tonight."

"Too busy?"

"Too sure I'd never have them."

"Adam didn't want kids?"

"He did. I just couldn't imagine ever being a mother. Mine was lousy at it. I figured I probably would be, too."

"And now?"

"I still think I'd be lousy at it, but at least I know I like kids." She grinned and snagged the cookie bag from Ben's hand. "You've had three. The last one is mine."

"I fought a pig for those cookies."

"And I wrangled a two-year-old into bed."

"Good point. The cookie is all yours."

"Thanks. Of course, I planned on eating it anyway." She pulled the cookie from the bag. "I'd better go check on Isaac and Honor."

He caught her hand before she could walk way, feeling

the delicate bones beneath her skin, the subtleness of her flesh. "Just so you know. I think you're wrong."

"About?"

"Being a mother. Personally, I think you'd make a great one."

She stared at him for just a moment, her eyes wide. Then her lips curved in a half smile. "Opal was saying the same thing to me a few days ago."

"Yeah?"

"Yeah. And I told her the same thing I'm going to tell you. Whether or not I'll be a good mother isn't an issue since I don't plan to ever get married."

"That's a shame." He stood, lifted a lock of her hair, let it slide through his fingers. "Because I think you'd make a good wife, too."

Her cheeks turned cherry red and she backed away. "I suppose I should say I'm glad you think so."

"But you're not going to?"

"Good guess. Now, I really do need to check on the kids." She hurried away and this time Ben let her go.

He probably shouldn't have mentioned Chloe having kids or getting married. Probably shouldn't have, but he didn't regret it. She was a woman who understood the value of family and relationships, and no matter how hard he tried, he couldn't imagine her living her life alone. What that meant as far as he was concerned, he didn't know.

Or maybe he did.

Maybe he just wasn't ready to accept it.

Eventually, though, he'd have to face the facts. His life had changed since he'd met Chloe, and unless he missed his guess, it was going to continue to change. God's plan was being worked out, the tide of events that had brought

Chloe into his life was leading them ever closer to a conclusion that hadn't yet been made clear.

Time.

That's all they needed.

Ben could only pray they'd get it.

TWENTY-THREE

Ben insisted on following Chloe home and, no matter her misgiving about their relationship, Chloe was happy for his company as she hurried across the yard. The new moon steeped the night in blackness and the silence seemed filled with danger, every soft sound amplified, every shadow sinister. She tried to ignore the fear that coursed through her as she stepped into the house and up the stairs, but it was like a living thing, wrapping around her lungs and stealing her breath.

If Ben noticed her anxiety, he didn't comment, just followed her up the stairs to her apartment. A package sat next to her door, and Chloe recognized it immediately. "Adam's hard drive. I was hoping it would come today."

She started to lift it, but Ben took it from her hands. "I'll get this. You get the door. It'll be easier that way."

"Thanks." She pushed the door open and flicked on the light, Abel's happy yips greeting her. "I'm coming, little guy—"

Ben pulled her to a stop before she could cross the room. "Why don't you wait here? I'll get the pup. He's in your room?"

"Yes. In his crate."

"Wait here." He didn't give her time to argue, and she didn't bother asking why he was walking through the small living room, pulling open the coat closet door, then stepping into the bathroom, ignoring Abel's unhappy cries.

She didn't have to ask. She knew why.

He was checking things out, making sure there wasn't anything or anyone unexpected waiting behind a closed door.

Just the thought of someone lurking behind the shower curtain or in a closet made her skin crawl. She stayed put as Ben stepped into her room and released Abel who bounded out to dance around her feet.

She lifted him and stepped across the living room and into her bedroom, watching as Ben pulled open the closet door. "I guess it's a good thing I've got a small place. It cuts down on the number of places someone can hide."

"I'm not too worried about someone hiding here, but it's always better to be sure."

He moved back out into the living room, pushed the curtains away from the balcony doors. They were still bolted shut against the darkness outside.

"It looks like everything is just as it should be."

He lifted the hard drive from the floor where he'd set it. "Where do you want this?"

"Over next to my computer, but I'll do it once I take the packaging off."

"Tell you what. While you do that, I'll bring Abel out."

"That's not necessary, Ben."

"Actually, it is." There was a hint of a smile in his eyes, but Chloe had no doubt he that he intended to do exactly what he suggested whether she protested or not.

He pulled the house keys from her hand, grabbed the

leash that was hanging from the knob and pushed open the door. "I'll be back in a few."

The door closed, the lock slid home, Chloe shook her head.

"Infuriating, exasperating man."

Strong, dependable man.

Attractive, loyal, intelligent man.

"You are *not* going to spend the next fifteen minutes listing all Ben's attributes. Do something constructive instead."

She tore the packaging from the hard drive, pulled the machine from the box. She'd helped Adam choose his PC more than a year ago when he'd upgraded from an outdated slower model. They'd purposely chosen a system that was compatible with Chloe's, thinking they'd be merging their lives. Now Adam was gone, but maybe some of who he'd been was left behind, easy to find in his e-mail accounts or perhaps hidden deep in the bowels of the hard drive. Whatever was there, Chloe would find it and she prayed that when she did, the shadowy stranger who haunted her dreams would be pulled into the light, that the nightmare she was living would be over.

But even that wouldn't bring Adam back.

Tears burned her eyes, but she ignored them, forcing herself to move instead, to focus her attention on the hard drive, on connecting it to her own system, typing in the password she'd created out of random letters and numbers. She only meant to make sure everything was working, but each keystroke brought her closer to solving the mystery and she was drawn deeper and deeper into the investigation.

Adam's e-mail account had been canceled a few months after his death. It didn't matter. The computer system hadn't been cleaned and anything that had been there was still there, begging to be found. She started typing, the sound of the front door opening and closing barely registering as she began her search.

"Coffee?" Ben's voice pulled her from the trail she'd been following and Chloe struggled to make sense of his question.

"What?"

"Want a cup of coffee? I've just brewed a pot."

Groggy and fuzzy-headed, Chloe stood, wincing as stiff muscles protested. "Maybe I will have some."

"Are you making any progress?"

"I've retrieved e-mails from the months before the accident and printed them out so I can read them more carefully. Right now, I'm not seeing anything unusual."

"What would be unusual?"

"Maybe if I knew it I'd find it." She accepted the cup Ben held out for her, rubbing a hand against the crick in her neck. "Computer forensics is a lot like searching for needles in haystacks. Lots and lots of stuff you don't want to find and only one thing you're really looking for."

"You love it, though."

She took a sip of coffee and met his eyes. "I do."

"But you're not doing it anymore. Why?"

"The accident made me reassess my life. I decided to move back to a place I loved and try something new for a living." Something that didn't remind her of the past and all its horrors.

"Maybe."

"Maybe what?"

"Maybe that's what you're telling yourself, but I'm not sure it's the truth." He stared at her through hooded eyes, his expression hidden.

"Then what do *you* think the truth is?"

"I think you're doing penance. Denying yourself a job you love because you think Adam's death is your fault."

"I don't need to be psychoanalyzed, Ben."

"That's good, because I don't know the first thing about doing it." He placed his coffee cup in the sink, shrugged on the jacket he must have taken off when he came back inside. "What I do know is that God has a purpose and plan for each of us. When we're living that, we find contentment and reason. When we're denying it, we can never be satisfied with what we accomplish."

"Are you saying you think I'm supposed to work with computers, not flowers?"

"I'm saying I've watched you do both and it's obvious to me which one you should be doing. I'm just not sure why it's not obvious to you. It's late. I'm going to head out." He pulled open the door and stepped out into the hall. "You know, you've got a skill not many people possess, Chloe. A tenacity and drive that allows you to search for answers relentlessly. It's a gift. One you're wasting in Opal's shop."

"It's not a gift. It's a job. One I've chosen not to do anymore."

"Too bad. There are a lot of people you could help, a lot of good you could do. Lock the door. I'll see you tomorrow at six." He strode away, and Chloe closed the door, shoving the bolt into place.

"He's wrong, Abel." She picked up the puppy, rubbed his head. "Just because I mutilated one flower arrangement doesn't mean I'm not cut out to be a florist. And just because I spent a few minutes—" she glanced at the clock "—an hour and a half in front of the computer without budging doesn't mean that's what I should spend my life doing."

Did it?

When she'd left D.C. she'd been running. From the nightmare, from her terror and memories. From her guilt. She'd thought leaving her old life behind would free her from those things. And maybe, as Ben had suggested, she'd thought denying herself the career she'd loved would serve as payment for the fact that she'd survived while Adam perished.

Penance.

It wasn't something she'd ever thought about, wasn't something she'd consciously sought to give, but maybe Ben was right. Maybe she *was* punishing herself, denying herself the career she'd worked so hard for, the skill she'd spent years honing because she couldn't bear the thought that her life stretched out before her while Adam's had been cut short.

Maybe.

But that wasn't the only reason she'd left her old life behind. When Ben had spoken of God's purpose and plan, the words had dug talons into her soul that closed tight and weren't letting go. Before the accident, she hadn't wondered what God thought of her career, her marriage plans, her day-to-day activities. She'd prayed, gone to church, tried to live her life with integrity. She just wasn't sure she'd lived it with purpose.

When she'd left D.C., that's what she'd been looking for. A chance to step back, take a clearer look at where she'd been, where she was going and how those things fit into God's will and plan. Slowly, it seemed she was finding the answers here in this quiet rural town with its tight-knit community and beautiful landscape. The longer she stayed in Lakeview the more she felt the truth. There *was* a correct path to take, a clear direction He had set for her. All she had to do was trust that it was for the best, that wherever it led, He'd be there.

And that was the hard part.

Faith. Believing in what couldn't be seen, trusting in something that could only sometimes be felt. Hoping in a future that sometimes seemed uncertain. "But I want to believe, Lord. I want to trust. I want to have faith that wherever You lead, I can go. That whatever happens, You're in control of it, working it out for the best. For *my* best."

A sense of peace filled her as she placed Abel on the floor and poured herself another cup of coffee. She might not know what the future would bring, she might not even know what tomorrow would bring, but she knew that it was all in God's hands. For now, that would have to be enough.

"Come on, Abel. We've got more files to discover."

A killer to uncover.

A job to do. A new life to create. One that might have more to do with computers than flowers. More to do with faith than work. More to do with trust than doubt.

More to do with God than self.

And that, Chloe thought, was going to be the biggest change of all.

TWENTY-FOUR

She found it at just past three in the morning. A deleted e-mail that chased fatigue from her body and brought her straight up in her seat, her heart thrumming with excitement. She printed it out, scanned the content one more time. Just three lines. Innocuous out of context, but in light of what had happened, a red flag.

You'll regret what you've done. Maybe not today or tomorrow, but eventually. Once you see the error of your ways, we'll talk. J.

J.?

Chloe could think of at least five of Adam's friends who had that name. Probably more. The message had been e-mailed from a free online account and contained no clue as to who the sender was. Chloe printed out the contents of Adam's address book, searching for the e-mail address and finding it. There was no contact information and no name listed. Chloe would have to give Jake the address and see if he could have the user information released from the e-mail provider.

An hour later, she was still at the computer, but hadn't

found any more e-mails from the same account. That seemed odd. Of course, everything seemed odd in the wee hours of the morning. Finally, she gave up, crawling into bed and staring up at the ceiling, praying for sleep that didn't want to come. When it did, Chloe's dreams were filled with troubling images. Not the nightmare. More a mishmash of faces and voices, identities and words that were just out of reach.

She woke more tired than when she'd gone to bed, grabbed a quick cup of coffee, then called Jake. He took down the e-mail address and promised to look into it immediately, but even that didn't seem fast enough. Like the images in her dreams, the answers they needed to find the stalker were just out of reach.

She glanced at the clock. Nine o'clock was early for anyone to be in Adam's old office, but she dialed the number anyway. James and Jordyn were both in for a few hours on Saturday. Hopefully, one of them would get back to her.

To her surprise, Jordyn answered the phone, her upbeat tone a little too bright after so few hours of sleep. "Kelly and Hill Investigations, how can I help you?"

"Jordyn, it's Chloe."

"You're calling early."

"I'm doing some research and need to get more information from you."

"Well, you're lucky you reached me. James is testifying on Monday. We're working on his testimony. Otherwise I wouldn't be in for several more hours."

"I'm glad things worked out."

"So, what do you need?"

"You've got a list of company contacts, right?"

"Yes, but that information is confidential."

"I don't need the whole list. I've got an e-mail address and I thought it might belong to one of Adam's clients. I was hoping you could check the list and see if the address matches anyone on the list."

"I don't know, Chloe. I'm not sure I'm allowed to do that. Why don't you give me the address and I'll check with James?"

"That's fine." Chloe rattled it off. "Can you please tell James this is really important?"

"I'll tell him, but I can't promise we'll be back to you with this before Monday."

"That's all right." Though it seemed like a long time to wait when she was so close to finding the information she'd been seeking.

"Good. By the way, did you get Adam's laptop, yet?"

"No, but hopefully it will come in today and I'll find some more e-mails from the address I just gave you."

"Good luck with that. Adam wasn't much for keeping old e-mails. He was always losing communications from clients and then having me call to have them resend the information. It used to drive me to distraction."

"Deleted e-mails are no problem, Jordyn. The information is still in the computer's memory, it's just hidden."

"Yes, well, you're the expert in those things. Not me. Good luck on your search and I'll get back to you once I speak to James."

Chloe hung up the phone and paced across the room. She had a lead, but nowhere to run with it. She'd have to wait until the laptop arrived, wait until Jordyn got back to her, wait until Jake was able to get the contact information from the e-mail account.

Wait.

"But I'm not so good at waiting, pup." She grabbed the leash from the door. "Let's take a quick walk. Then maybe we should get out for a while. Run to the pet store. Get some groceries. Hopefully, when we get back I'll have some more ideas about tracing the person who's using that address."

A few hours of shopping hadn't given Chloe any clearer insight into the problem. It *had* filled her cupboards, though, and when the phone rang at a little past noon, she was putting together a grilled cheese sandwich and a salad.

"Hello?"

"Chloe, it's Ben."

Chloe's heart leaped at his voice. "Hi. What's up?"

"Cain. He's racing around the house like a sugar-hyped kid. I thought maybe it was time for that playdate."

"I don't know."

"You're busy?"

"Having lunch."

"Maybe I could join you."

"You're inviting yourself for lunch?"

"It's easier than waiting for an invitation."

Chloe laughed. "I'm not a fancy cook. Grilled cheese and salad."

"I'll bring dessert. See you in ten."

He made it in seven, the cool, crisp scent of autumn drifting into the apartment as he strode through the door, a brown paper bag in one hand, Cain dancing around his feet. "You look tired."

"Is that the way you greet every woman you have lunch with or am I just special?"

"You're definitely special." He smiled, but there was a hint of truth in his words and in the somber gaze he swept over her. "How long did you stay up last night?"

"Long enough to find what I was looking for." She grabbed the printed e-mail and handed it to Ben. "Tell me what you think while I grill the sandwiches."

He read it quickly, his expression darkening. "Did you call Jake?"

"First thing this morning. He's going to try and get the e-mail provider to release the account holder's contact information."

"Which may or may not be useful."

"True, but I'm hoping I'll find a few more e-mails on Adam's laptop. Maybe contact information in his address book. That will definitely be useful."

"And that'll be here when?"

"Probably today or Monday. I'm hoping for today."

"Me, too. The sooner we get this solved, the better I'll feel." He frowned, staring down at the e-mail as if he could find the sender's identity hidden in the message. "This could be about anything business or personal."

"And it might not have anything to do with the accident or the break-in or the phone calls Adam received, but look at the date on it. That's just a couple of days after Adam and I broke up. I think that's significant."

"It's a start, anyway."

"Yeah. Hopefully of something big." Chloe placed grilled cheese sandwiches on a platter, salad in a bowl and set both on the table. "I'm ready for all this to be over."

"Have you decided what you're going to do when it is?"

"I can't think past today. When everything is settled, I'll plan for more."

Ben nodded, not asking the questions Chloe could see in his eyes. "We'd better eat and get these dogs outside. Cain needs to run off some energy."

The walk was pleasant, though Chloe was sure Ben was as distracted as she was, conversation that had always seemed to flow so easily when she was with him, felt stilted and strange.

"Is something wrong?" She asked the question as they moved back up the stairs to her apartment. "You're quiet today."

He met her gaze, his eyes the vivid blue of the sky in spring. "I'm worried. We've got bits and pieces of the puzzle, but not enough to see the picture clearly. Whoever is after you must realize how close we're getting."

"I don't think he cares."

"Which worries me even more." He raked a hand through his hair and frowned. "Maybe you should leave town for a while."

"Where would I go? My friends are all in D.C. I haven't heard from my mother or grandmother in years."

"Anywhere where you can stay hidden until this is over. My parents. One of my foster siblings. They'd be willing to take you in."

"But I'm not willing to go. I've been running for almost a year. I won't run anymore." She meant it. Despite the fear, despite the nightmare, she couldn't keep running. Not if she ever wanted to have the life she dreamed of, the peace she longed for.

The muscle in Ben's jaw tightened, but he nodded. "I can understand that. I even respect it. But I don't like it."

"I'll be careful, Ben. I'm not planning to make myself any more vulnerable than I already am." She hesitated, then wrapped her arms around his waist, hugging him close for just a moment before she stepped away.

"What was that for?"

"For caring. There haven't been that many people in my life who have."

"I care, Chloe." He leaned forward, brushed his lips against hers. "And when you're ready, maybe we'll discuss just how much. I've got to go. We've got a prayer meeting at the church. Then I've got to run to the hospital to visit a sick friend. How about I come by and pick you up and we go to Opal's together?"

"Sure."

He smiled. "I think this is the first time I've offered to help that you haven't argued. We're making progress. I'll see you."

The apartment was silent in the wake of his departure, Chloe's heart beating just a little faster than normal. She pressed a finger against her lips, sure she could still feel his warmth there.

She'd come to Lakeview hoping to find peace and safety, but it seemed she'd found a lot more—community, friendship, contentment. Ben. Faith, first budding, then blooming, filling her heart, telling her that no matter what happened, everything would be okay.

TWENTY-FIVE

The mail carrier knocked on her door at three, the short quick rap against the wood startling Chloe from the half-sleep she'd fallen into.

Excitement, anticipation and fear coursed through her as she tore open the box and set the laptop up on her kitchen table.

As Jordyn had said, most of Adam's e-mails had been deleted. Chloe checked the address book, found it empty, and frowned. Adam might have deleted e-mails, but would he have deleted the contents of his address book?

She didn't think so.

But someone else might have. Someone who had something to hide. James? Jordyn? Had one of them been embezzling funds? Or doing something else illegal that Adam had uncovered? If so, why sabotage Chloe's car? Why come after her?

She didn't have the answers, but Chloe hoped she'd find them. *Prayed* she'd find them.

First, she grabbed the phone, called Jake again, this time leaving a message on his voice mail. She knew her thoughts were rambling and unclear, her words unfocused, but her mind was already racing forward, following paths and trails through the computer files, hurrying toward the key to everything that had happened.

She searched for two hours, printing out copies of deleted e-mails, scanning through them, coming up blank time and time again.

"It's in here. I know it is." She stood and stretched, her thigh screaming in protest, her muscles cramped from too many hours spent in front of the computer, frustration thrumming through her. Whatever was imbedded in the computer was going to have to remain there for another hour or so. She had Checkers to feed, Opal's mail to check.

The thought of calling Ben and asking him to do both by himself flitted through her mind, but she pushed it aside. An hour away from the computer would do her good, clear her mind. So would talking to Ben. Maybe he could come in afterward, read through the files she'd already printed, see if anything struck him as off.

"Good excuse for inviting him over, Chloe." She mumbled the words, then lifted Abel. "Sorry, guy. You're going to have to stay home this time. But I'll take you out for a little while now to make up for it." She grabbed her purse and keys and headed outside.

Evening had come, painting the sky deep purple, the trees and grass gray. Chloe shivered from the chill and from the fear that she could never quite leave behind. She wouldn't let it beat her though, wouldn't go back inside and lock herself into the apartment, hide her head under the pillows.

But maybe she should have.

As she moved down the steps and out into the yard, Abel barked, darting toward a shadow that was separating from the trees. A woman. Above average height. Blond hair. Very familiar.

And suddenly very frightening, the wild look in her blue eyes telling Chloe all she needed to know about Adam's receptionist.

She forced down fear and panic, took a step back toward the house. "Jordyn. What are you doing here?"

"I'm sure you already know."

"You got the information from James and brought it for me?" Chloe took another step back as she spoke, moving away from the tree line and toward the house, her hand sliding toward her pocket and the pepper spray she carried there.

"Don't play stupid, Chloe. It's an insult to Adam and his taste in women." She pulled something from her pocket and pointed it at Chloe. The tiny gun looked more like a toy than a weapon. "And while you're at it, stop trying to get back to your apartment. That older couple who's always coming and going might not look so cute with bullets in their heads."

Chloe blanched at the words, but did as Jordyn commanded, stopping short, her heart hammering a frantic rhythm. One swift movement and she'd have the pepper spray in her hand, but first she needed to be close enough to use it.

The panic button!

Her hand slid over the zipper of her purse. Why had she put the keys in it when she'd locked the door?

"Drop the purse, Chloe. Now."

Die now or stay alive and hope for escape?

There was no choice, and Chloe dropped the purse.

Jordyn smiled, the cold wildness in her eyes making Chloe shiver. "That's better. Now, keep your hand out of your pocket. I'm sure you're still carrying around pepper spray. You would have been smart to get something a little more deadly." She waved the gun. "It's too late now, though, isn't it?"

"What's going on, Jordyn?"

"What do you *think* is going on? I've come for a visit to see how you're holding up. Losing Adam must have been so devastating for you. Of course, since he was never really yours, I guess you can't complain."

"What do you want?"

"Revenge."

"For what?"

"For what you did to Adam, of course. What he and I had was special. You ruined it. Then you killed him."

"I didn't kill him."

"Of course you did." She spit the words out, moving a step closer.

Come on. Keep coming.

Just a few steps closer and Chloe would take a chance and go for the pepper spray.

"If you hadn't brought that information to the FBI, Adam would still be alive."

"Then it wasn't you who sabotaged my car?" Keep her talking. Keep her moving forward.

"Maybe you really *are* stupid. Matthew Jackson wanted you dead. It would have made me very happy for you to end up that way. But I didn't do anything to your car. I have more subtle ways of getting rid of people who stand in my way." She smiled, her teeth flashing white in the fading light. "Take the pepper spray out of your pocket. Throw it into the trees."

Chloe hesitated.

"Now, Chloe, or those sweet old people will be vulture food."

Chloe did as she was told, her muscles tight and ready for action. If only she knew what action to take.

"By the way, I wanted to tell you when we chatted just how much I love your place. Very cute. Very quaint. Very you. Now, come on. We have to go before the newest man in your life shows up and makes me go to more effort than I already have."

"Go where?"

"To finish what I started in D.C. I thought dissolving those pills in that bit of orange juice you had in your fridge would take care of things, but you managed to survive. Too bad. Overdosing wouldn't have been such a bad way to die."

"Look, Jordyn—"

"You look, Chloe. I played second fiddle to you for years, knowing that eventually Adam would come back to me. He did. Just as he was supposed to. Then you ruined everything. I'm sure guilt is eating you alive. It's time to put an end to your misery. And mine."

"Whatever you're planning won't work. I already told the police that I thought you or James might be responsible for everything that's been happening."

"But you're crazy, Chloe. Everyone in D.C. knows it. Since Adam's death, it's obvious the trauma was too much for you to deal with. All those night terrors in the hospital, your insistence that someone was after you. It was only a matter of time before you cracked."

"Things are different here."

"Are they? You think that because you've got some good-looking pastor hanging around and a sheriff who seems to be taking you seriously that no one will believe it when your suicide note is found? I've got news for you, Chloe, people believe whatever is easiest. Get in the car."

"There'll be an investigation, Jordyn, and you'll be one of the top suspects."

"I doubt it, but even if I am, they won't be able to prove anything. They'll have your suicide note, but no body. No evidence to link the two of us together. Nothing that a prosecutor would be willing to bring to trial, anyway. Do you know how many killers are free because there's simply no evidence to link them to the crime? Now get in the car. We've got places to go."

No way. Gun or no gun, Chloe wasn't getting in the car, she pivoted, the sharp movement sending pain shooting up her thigh. Her leg collapsed out from under her and she stumbled, tried to right herself. Something slammed into her head, stars burst in front of her eyes and she was falling into darkness and into the nightmare.

Chloe wasn't answering the door and she hadn't answered her phone. It was possible she was in the apartment, caught up in the investigation and oblivious to the world. Ben had seen her in action, watched her fingers fly across the keyboard. Doing so had been a surprise and revelation, had told him a lot more than Chloe's words just how much she needed to be back at her work.

Maybe she was working now, bent over the computer, intent, focused. Maybe. But he didn't think so. What he thought was that Chloe was gone. The fact that her car was still parked in the driveway could only mean one thing—trouble.

He dialed Jake's number as he strode back outside, praying that he was wrong, knowing that he was right and hoping that he and Jake would be able to find Chloe in time.

Chloe woke to icy terror and throbbing pain, water filling her nose and throat. The urge to gasp for breath, to suck in liquid in hopes of finding air nearly overwhelmed her. Darkness beneath, darkness above, something tied to her legs and pulling her down. She fought against it, pushing upward, out of the water, gasping for air, sucking in huge heaving breaths, the sickening pain in her head worsening with the movement.

She blinked, trying to clear her vision, caught a glimpse of wood, an oar. Saw Jordyn staring down at her, watching through glassy eyes.

"You just won't die will you?" She lifted the oar, swinging hard.

Chloe ducked back under the water, the weight on her legs dragging her down farther than she expected. She tried to keep her buoyancy, but sank deep, the darkness of the water profound, her lungs screaming in protest.

More fighting, more struggling, until finally she broke the surface of the water again. The boat was farther away now, the quiet slap of the oar hitting the water the only sound Chloe could hear. It was near dark, the hazy purple of dusk deepening to blue-black, the crisp day turning frigid with night. Chloe shivered, sank back under the water again, choking. Gasping. Sliding into darkness. She flailed, the cold and the weight on her legs sapping her energy, stealing her strength. She struggled back up again, tried to swim toward shore and sank again.

If you want to live, you'd better stop panicking and think, Chloe.

The thought pierced through her terror. Think or die. It was as simple as that.

She let herself sink into the water, reaching down to feel whatever it was that was dragging her down. Thick rope wrapped her ankles together, pulled taut by something.

What? A weight? An anchor? She pulled hard on the rope, yanking the object up until she was holding what felt like a cinder block. Then she pushed to the surface again, just managing to suck in a breath of air before she sank beneath the water again. Her vision swam, her stomach heaved and she almost lost her grip on the weight and on consciousness. She bit the inside of her cheek, the pain clearing her head as she struggled back out of the water again.

Where was the shore? Where was safety?

In the dim light the shore looked too far away, the house in the distance tiny and insubstantial. To the left, the lake stretched as far as Chloe could see. To the right, trees shot up at the shoreline, distant and unreachable. Still, if her legs were free, she could swim to safety easily enough.

If.

Jake hopped out of his car and strode toward Ben, his stride long and stiff, his face grim. "Any sign of her?"

"No, but I found her puppy hiding under her car."

"Not good." The sympathy and worry in Jake's gaze was obvious. "When was the last time you spoke to her?"

"Around noon." Ben ran a hand over his jaw, forcing himself to think clearly, to stay focused. "I've already walked the perimeter of the house twice. The earth's too dry to hold prints."

"Did you talk to her neighbors?"

"I tried. They weren't home." Ben surveyed the area, urgency pounding through him, demanding action. "Something's happened to her."

"I've called in all my off-duty officers. We'll work a grid from here to the lake and the road. If she's here, we'll find her."

"And if she's not?"

"We'll contact media, get her picture out there. Pray that somebody's seen her."

"I've been doing that. Now I want to act."

"Understood, but we go traipsing around without a plan and we'll waste time, maybe destroy evidence." Jake's phone rang and he answered, his jaw tight, his words terse. "Reed, here. Yeah. I'll check it out. Thanks."

"What's up?"

"Guy a half a mile from here was walking his dog and found a boat washed up in the reeds near his house. He said there's some stuff inside of it. A purse. Flowers. It seemed strange so he called it in."

"Let's go."

"Maybe I should take this one myself."

"Maybe not. Let's go." Ben strode toward the cruiser, fear a hard knot in his chest. Chloe was somewhere nearby. He felt that as surely as he felt that she was in danger. They had to find her. Soon.

They took the cruiser, racing the half mile to a long tree-lined driveway and a two-story home that looked out over the lake. The man who met them seemed shaken as he led them down to the water. There was no dock, just thick weed-choked grass and slick rocks. A boat bobbed in the water, white lilies on its water-logged bottom, a purse lying on its side the contents spilling out.

"When did you first notice this?" Jake spoke as he moved toward the boat.

"Just a few minutes ago. I saw it when I let the dog out. It wasn't here when I got home an hour ago."

"And did you see anyone out here? Hear anything?"

"Nothing. It's just been a regular day." The man ran a

hand over sparse hair. "I might not have thought that much about the boat, but the flowers and purse worried me."

"They worry me, too. I'm glad you called." Jake pulled on gloves, grabbed the bow of the boat and dragged it up over the rocks and onto shore. "There's a paper here. Looks like a note." He picked it up, holding it gingerly, his face hardening as he read. "We've got a problem."

"We already had one."

"It's just gotten worse." He gestured Ben over, holding the note out for him to see. The words were smudged but easy to read.

"A suicide note."

"*Chloe's* suicide note."

"Written by someone else." Ben shoved the boat back toward the water.

"We need to get other transportation. That boat could contain evidence."

"We don't have time to find another boat." Ben gritted his teeth and stared his friend down. He was going out on the lake, with or without Jake. With or without his approval.

Finally, Jake nodded. "Let's go."

A few minutes of swimming with the cinder block in her arm convinced Chloe that she'd be better off expending her energy in another way. First she tried feeling for the ends of the rope, hoping she might be able to untie it, but each time she stopped paddling with her free arm, she dipped under the water.

"That's not going to work, Chloe. Come up with something else." She spoke out loud, the words sputtering and gasping into air and water, her teeth chattering. "Lord, if there's some way out of this, I hope you'll show me quickly because I don't know how much longer I can do this."

But there didn't seem to be a way out, just one painful stroke after another toward a way-too-distant shore. Chloe's head throbbed with each movement, her body telling her to quit while her mind screamed for her to keep going. She slipped under the water, choking and gagging as she surfaced again, the rope wrapping around her wrist and sliding over her skin.

Sliding over her skin.

The thought worked its way past her pain and fatigue, and she reached down, tried to shove the rope past her jeans. It moved. Not much, but enough to give her hope. One handed wasn't going to work though. She'd have to let go of the cinder block. Use both hands to shove the rope down. Once she did that, she'd be pulled back down toward the bottom of the lake. If she failed, she didn't know if she'd be able to fight her way back up again.

Unfortunately, her choices were limited and so was her time.

"Lord, I trust you. Whatever happens, I know you're with me." With that, she let go of the cement block, grabbed the rope that was wrapped around her legs and started to push it down as she sank deeper into the water. The rope pulled tight, so tight she couldn't get her fingers between it and her legs. Panic speared through her, but she forced it back, trying again, feeling fingernails bend and skin tear as she finally made room between rope and denim. Pull. Tug. Push. Yank. Muscles quivering. Head pounding. Fear like she'd only ever known once before. The nightmare, but different. Not fire and hot metal. Water and burning lungs. Blackness outside and inside. Alone.

But not alone.

God had not abandoned her. Would not abandon her.

The rope moved, inching down toward her ankles, scraping past her jeans. She yanked the fabric up with one hand, shoving the rope down, feeling it give. Then she was free, floating up toward the surface, her lungs ready to explode, the desperate need for oxygen making her want to gasp and breathe and hope for the best.

She broke the surface of the lake, coughing and gasping, her body trembling with fatigue and with cold. She had to swim, but her movements were clumsy, her efforts weak.

She wasn't going to give up, though. She wasn't going to quit. She was going to get out of the lake and she was going to make sure Jordyn was arrested for her crimes.

Her energy and attention were focused on the goal—a distant light that she was sure must be home. What she wasn't sure about was whether or not she was actually getting any closer to it.

Suddenly the light disappeared, a dark shape appearing in front of Chloe. For a moment, her muddled thoughts conjured a monster rising up from the depth of the lake. Then the truth of what she was seeing registered—a boat.

Jordyn. She was sure it was the same boat. Sure that Jordyn would lean over the edge, raise the oar, slam it down into the water. Or worse. Take out the gun and shoot her.

She turned, trying to swim away, her arms flailing, her muscles giving out. She sank. Surfaced. Sank again.

"Chloe!" The shout carried over the splash and gasp of her frantic attempt to escape.

An arm hooked around her waist and she was pulled back against a hard chest. "Stop struggling, Chloe. I've got you."

Ben.

His voice rumbled in her ear, his body warming her, but doing nothing to ease the shivers that racked her body.

"Are you okay?"

She nodded, but her teeth were chattering too hard to get the words out.

"Here she comes, Jake."

Before Chloe knew what was happening, she was out of Ben's arms and in a boat, a leather jacket draped around her shoulders, Jake Reed flashing a light in her face. "You hurt anywhere?"

"My head." The words rasped out as Ben pulled himself into the boat. "Jordyn hit me with something. Maybe her gun."

"Jordyn Winslow? That's one of the names you gave me earlier."

"Yes, Adam's receptionist." She was still shivering, her muscles so tight with cold she wasn't sure she'd ever be warm again.

Ben pulled her toward him, rubbed her arms briskly, the heat he generated speeding through her body. "Better?"

"Yes." But not because she was warmer. Because he was there, warm, solid, steady.

He ran a hand over the back of her head, probing the tender flesh there. "You're bleeding. Can you call for an ambulance, Jake?"

"There's no—"

"There's no sense arguing. You're going to the hospital."

"I'm not much for hospitals. My experiences there haven't been pleasant."

"Maybe not in the past, but this time will be different. This time I'll be with you." Ben's words were a warm caress against her ear and Chloe relaxed back into his arms, allowing herself to believe what she hadn't in a very long time—that she was safe and that everything was going to be all right.

TWENTY-SIX

"Fifteen stitches does not make me an invalid, Opal." Chloe smiled as she spoke, accepting the bowl of chicken noodle soup Opal handed her.

"Fifteen stitches *and* a concussion. The doctor said you should take it easy."

"And I have been."

"How does starting back up in computer forensics constitute resting?"

"I haven't done any work. I've just been contacting old clients and letting them know I will be."

"Yes, well, I still have to decide if I forgive you for that. You were doing so well at Blooming Baskets."

Chloe would have laughed if she wasn't sure it would send pain shooting through her head. "Opal, I have as much artistic vision as a rock and you know it."

"Okay, so flowers weren't the perfect fit for you."

"But computers are."

"Apparently so. And you know that I'm happy if you are. If computers are what you're meant to do, far be it from me to try to keep you from them." Opal leaned forward and kissed her cheek. "Now, I've really got to get home. Checkers is still angry about not being fed on time Saturday night."

"Maybe if you explained that I was fighting for my life and kind of distracted, he'll forgive me."

"Doubtful. Call me if you need something."

"I will." Chloe started to rise, but froze when Opal sent a searing look in her direction.

"Do not get up from there. At all."

Before Chloe could respond, a soft knock sounded on the door. "Good. Now I really can leave." Opal hurried to the door and pulled it open. "You're late."

"Two minutes. And I had good reason." Ben stepped into the room, a white paper bag in his hand. "Apple pie and ice cream from Becky's."

"I suppose that's acceptable. I'll be back in an hour or so. Thanks for taking over for me."

"Opal, please tell me you didn't ask Ben to come babysit me."

"I did not ask him to babysit you. I asked him to lend a hand. I'll see you in a bit." She walked out the door before Chloe could tell her exactly what she thought of her meddling ways.

"Feeling better?" Ben sat on the couch beside her, his gaze taking in everything about her appearance.

Unfortunately, that included scraggly hair, pale skin, swollen hands and, of course, plenty of stitches.

"Now that Jordyn is in custody, I feel better than I have in almost a year. I still can't believe she went home and was acting like nothing happened. I was sure she'd take off and go into hiding."

"From what Jake says, she'd convinced herself that no one would suspect her. In her mind, she'd committed the perfect crime."

"Except I didn't die."

"Thank the Lord for that." Ben ran a hand over his jaw, his eyes shadowed. "I was sure we'd lost you when I saw that suicide note."

"I guess I'm tougher than you think."

"I've always thought you were tough. I was just afraid whoever had you was tougher."

"Jordyn did pack a pretty mean punch." Chloe fingered the bandage at the back of her head. "She really was crazy, Ben. I found e-mails in Adam's laptop—"

"What were you doing working when you're supposed to be resting?"

"I just took a quick peek."

"How long of a quick peek?"

"A couple of hours."

"That's what I thought." Ben chuckled, his hand resting on her shoulder, his finger warm against her neck. "So, what did you find?"

"That Jordyn thought she and Adam were going to be together forever. She's been in love with him for years."

"Was she the other woman?"

"I think so. From what I gathered, they went out a few times years ago. Then seemed to reconnect for a while, during the months before Adam died. She proclaimed her love for him over and over again in her e-mails."

"And scared him away?"

"Knowing Adam, yes." She shrugged. "The most recent e-mails, the ones she sent right before he died, were mostly hateful rantings. She threatened me a few times. Told him that if he got back together with me, we'd both be sorry."

"Did you show Jake?"

"Yeah, he's already come by for the e-mails and taken

the laptop in as evidence. He mentioned something that surprised me."

"What's that?"

"He thinks there might be a connection between Jordyn and Matthew Jackson. I was freelancing for James when I worked on The Strangers case. There's a good possibility Jordyn somehow made contact with one of the group's members, maybe hoping she'd find someone who wanted to get me out of the way. There's no proof that's what happened, but it makes sense."

"If he's right that might have been enough to send her over the edge. If she thought she'd get rid of you, but it backfired and Adam was killed—"

"She would have gone a little crazy. Guilt can be a terrible thing."

"I'm not sure she was capable of guilt, but she did corner the market on hate."

"I wish…" Chloe's voice trailed off and she shook her head, not sure what she wished, what she wanted.

"That you could have known?"

"Yes, but even that wouldn't have saved Adam."

Ben pulled her into his arms, his hands smoothing down her back and resting at her waist. "No, it wouldn't have, but you can't spend your life thinking about that, Chloe."

"I know." She blinked hard, trying to force back tears. They refused to be stopped and slid down her cheeks, dripping onto Ben's shirt.

He brushed away the moisture, his palm warm against her skin. "Are you crying for Adam?"

"He never even had a chance."

"But you do. A chance at life. At friendship. At love. Adam wouldn't want you to pass that up."

At love?

Chloe looked up into his eyes, felt herself pulled in again. Into his confidence. His strength. Into all the things she'd wanted for so long, but was sure she'd never have.

"You're right. He wouldn't. And I don't want to pass those things up, either."

His lips curved, the slow, easy smile tugging at Chloe's heart. "That makes two of us."

He leaned forward, kissing her with passion and with promise, chasing the nightmare away and replacing it with a dream of the future spent with a man who shared her faith, her goals, her heart. A man put into her life by God. A gift that Chloe would always be thankful for.

EPILOGUE

The dark night pressed in around her, the sound of laughter and music a backdrop to the wild beating of her heart. Chloe shoved a box of floral decorations out of the way and reached for her suitcase and the small bag of clothes sitting beside it, the heady aroma of hyacinth drifting on the air and filling her with longing and with joy. This was it, then. A new beginning. A new dream. A new life.

She was ready for it.

"Need a hand?" The words were warm and filled with humor, the dark figure that stepped from the shadows stealing her breath.

"Maybe more than one. I thought I'd put the suitcase into your car, but Tiffany and Opal helped me pack and I'm not sure I can handle it while I'm wearing heels."

"Then let me handle it for you." Ben's arms slipped around her waist, pulling her backward. She turned, staring up into his face, wanting to memorize this moment, the way she felt standing in his arms.

He smiled, caressing her shoulder, his fingers gliding over her skin, trailing heat with every touch. "Have I told you how beautiful you look today?"

"A hundred times."

"Then this will be a hundred and one. You're beautiful, Chloe. So beautiful you take my breath away." He trailed kisses up her neck, his hand cupping the back of her head, his body warm against hers.

"I was just thinking the same about you."

"That I'm beautiful?" His laughter rumbled near her ear.

"That you take my breath away." Chloe sank into his embrace, her love for Ben strong and sure and undeniable. "And that if we keep this up we may not make our flight."

"I'm not sure that would be such a bad thing."

"Me, neither." She tilted her head as his lips caressed the sensitive flesh beneath her jaw.

"So maybe we should go to my place and forget the airport." His eyes gleamed in the moonlight, dark and filled with promise.

"There you are." Opal bustled across the parking lot, salt and pepper curls bouncing with each step. "I thought you were changing into your traveling suit and coming right back to the reception."

"I got sidetracked."

"So I see, but if you two plan on making that flight to Thailand, you'd better get moving."

Ben met Chloe's gaze, the joy, the hope that she felt reflected in his eyes. "I'll get the suitcase into the car."

"I'll get changed."

"And I'll have everybody ready and waiting to say goodbye and throw rose petals. Five minutes. And don't make me come looking for you again."

Chloe smiled, following Opal back into the church and closing herself into Ben's office, her *husband's* office. She'd lived through so much heartache, so many tears, but those were in the past. Today was for new beginnings, fresh starts. Laughter. Joy. Peace.

A soft knock sounded at the door, and Chloe opened it, her heart skipping a beat as she caught sight of Ben. He'd changed into jeans and a polo shirt, his sandy hair falling over his forehead, his eyes gleaming brilliant blue. "Ready?"

"Absolutely."

"Then let's get started on the rest of our lives." He wrapped an arm around her waist, led her into the reception hall. His foster parents were there, standing beside the door with a dozen or more of his foster siblings. His sister Raven and her husband, Shane, were there, too. Opal. Sam. Tiffany and Jake. Hawke and Miranda.

So many people, so much happiness.

Chloe's heart welled with it, her eyes filling as white rose petals fell like gentle spring rain, washing over her, washing through her as Ben swept her into his arms and carried her into the future.

* * * * *

Dear Reader,

Faith isn't always easy. Often we wonder how things can be going so badly when we're trying so hard to trust God, serve Him and seek His will. The answer is as simple as it is complicated. God never promised that our lives would be free of pain and troubles. He only promised that whatever we're going through, He'll be with us through it. That's a lesson Chloe Davidson must learn as she begins a new life in Lakeview, Virginia, and faces some of the most difficult times of her life.

I hope you enjoy reading her story, and I pray that whatever troubles you may be going through, you'll have peace that can only come from the One who truly understands.

I love to hear from readers. You can contact me at Shirlee@shirleemccoy.com, or 1121 Annapolis Road, PMB 244, Odenton, Maryland, 21113-1633.

Blessings,

Shirlee McCoy

QUESTIONS FOR DISCUSSION

1. Chloe leaves her old life in Washington, D.C., to begin a new one in Lakeview. Why? What is she running from? Have you ever run from an uncomfortable situation?

2. As she settles into a new routine, Chloe can't help but be drawn into the lives of the people who live in Lakeview. How does she feel about belonging to a new community?

3. Chloe has a lot of fears that stem from the night her ex-fiancé, Adam, died. She seems to feel that her terror makes her weak. Do you think that is true? What are her strengths and weaknesses?

4. Ben is drawn to Chloe immediately. How does his view of her differ from Chloe's view of herself? How does his confidence in Chloe help her regain confidence in herself?

5. Ben is a widower who loved his late wife. When he meets Chloe, he's not looking for relationship. What is it about Chloe that makes him change his mind?

6. Chloe and Ben are attracted to each other immediately, but that isn't what draws them closer. What makes them a good match? In what way does this reflect God's plan for every relationship?

7. Struggles are part of life. During those struggles we can grow closer to God, or further away from Him. What happened to Chloe after the accident? What happened to Ben after his wife died?

8. Chloe makes an effort to get to know some of the townspeople by attending the church's quilting group. Have you ever taken that first step and been happy with the result? Unhappy? Why?

9. God has a plan for each of our lives. Sometimes that plan is easy to see. Sometimes it's not. How does Chloe find the strength to trust in God's plan when she doesn't understand it?

10. What struggles are you going through? How can you lean more fully on God's grace as you face these trials?

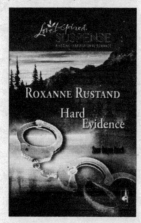

REQUEST YOUR FREE BOOKS!
2 FREE RIVETING INSPIRATIONAL NOVELS
PLUS 2 FREE MYSTERY GIFTS

Love Inspired®
SUSPENSE

YES! Please send me 2 FREE Love Inspired® Suspense novels and my 2 FREE mystery gifts. After receiving them, if I don't wish to receive any more books, I can return the shipping statement marked "cancel." If I don't cancel, I will receive 4 brand-new novels every month and be billed just $3.99 per book in the U.S. or $4.74 per book in Canada, plus 25¢ shipping and handling per book and applicable taxes, if any*. That's a savings of 20% off the cover price! I understand that accepting the 2 free books and gifts places me under no obligation to buy anything. I can always return a shipment and cancel at any time. Even if I never buy another book from Steeple Hill, the two free books and gifts are mine to keep forever.

123 IDN EL5H   323 IDN ELQH

Name	(PLEASE PRINT)

Address	Apt. #

City	State/Prov.	Zip/Postal Code

Signature (if under 18, a parent or guardian must sign)

Order online at www.LoveInspiredSuspense.com

Or mail to Steeple Hill Reader Service™:

IN U.S.A.: P.O. Box 1867, Buffalo, NY 14240-1867
IN CANADA: P.O. Box 609, Fort Erie, Ontario L2A 5X3

Not valid to current Love Inspired Suspense subscribers.

Want to try two free books from another series?
Call 1-800-873-8635 or visit www.morefreebooks.com

* Terms and prices subject to change without notice. NY residents add applicable sales tax. Canadian residents will be charged applicable provincial taxes and GST. This offer is limited to one order per household. All orders subject to approval. Credit or debit balances in a customer's account(s) may be offset by any other outstanding balance owed by or to the customer. Please allow 4 to 6 weeks for delivery.

Your Privacy: Steeple Hill is committed to protecting your privacy. Our Privacy Policy is available online at www.eHarlequin.com or upon request from the Reader Service. From time to time we make our lists of customers available to reputable firms who may have a product or service of interest to you. If you would prefer we not share your name and address, please check here: ☐

LISUS07

Love Inspired
SUSPENSE

TITLES AVAILABLE NEXT MONTH

Don't miss these four stories in December

HER CHRISTMAS PROTECTOR by Terri Reed

Running from her abusive ex-husband, Faith Delange found shelter in Sisters, Oregon. But how secure was her haven? The longer she stayed, the more she endangered her new friends, including protective rancher Luke Campbell.

BURIED SINS by Marta Perry
The Three Sisters Inn

Caroline Hampton feared her husband was involved in something shady, but he died before she could confront him...didn't he? A string of dangerous incidents implied otherwise. Caroline fled to her sisters' inn, but trouble—and the suspicions of Police Chief Zachary Burkhalter—followed her home....

HARD EVIDENCE by Roxanne Rustand
Snow Canyon Ranch

Human remains were found behind the isolated cabins Janna McAllister was fixing up on her family ranch. And she suspected someone lurked out there even still. Her unexpected lodger, Deputy Sheriff Michael Robertson, made the single mother feel safe. Until she unwittingly tempted a killer out of the woodwork.

BLUEGRASS PERIL by Virginia Smith

When her boss was murdered, the police suspected single mom Becky Dennison. To clear her name, Becky teamed up with Scott Lewis, from a neighboring breeder's farm, to find the truth. In this Kentucky race, the stakes were life or death.

LISCNM1107

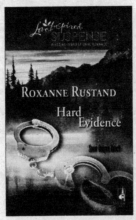

REQUEST YOUR FREE BOOKS!

2 FREE RIVETING INSPIRATIONAL NOVELS PLUS 2 FREE MYSTERY GIFTS

Love Inspired®
SUSPENSE

YES! Please send me 2 FREE Love Inspired® Suspense novels and my 2 FREE mystery gifts. After receiving them, if I don't wish to receive any more books, I can return the shipping statement marked "cancel." If I don't cancel, I will receive 4 brand-new novels every month and be billed just $3.99 per book in the U.S. or $4.74 per book in Canada, plus 25¢ shipping and handling per book and applicable taxes, if any*. That's a savings of 20% off the cover price! I understand that accepting the 2 free books and gifts places me under no obligation to buy anything. I can always return a shipment and cancel at any time. Even if I never buy another book from Steeple Hill, the two free books and gifts are mine to keep forever.

123 IDN EL5H 323 IDN ELQH

Name	(PLEASE PRINT)	
Address		Apt. #
City	State/Prov.	Zip/Postal Code

Signature (if under 18, a parent or guardian must sign)

Order online at www.LoveInspiredSuspense.com

Or mail to Steeple Hill Reader Service™:

IN U.S.A.: P.O. Box 1867, Buffalo, NY 14240-1867
IN CANADA: P.O. Box 609, Fort Erie, Ontario L2A 5X3

Not valid to current Love Inspired Suspense subscribers.

Want to try two free books from another series?
Call 1-800-873-8635 or visit www.morefreebooks.com

* Terms and prices subject to change without notice. NY residents add applicable sales tax. Canadian residents will be charged applicable provincial taxes and GST. This offer is limited to one order per household. All orders subject to approval. Credit or debit balances in a customer's account(s) may be offset by any other outstanding balance owed by or to the customer. Please allow 4 to 6 weeks for delivery.

Your Privacy: Steeple Hill is committed to protecting your privacy. Our Privacy Policy is available online at www.eHarlequin.com or upon request from the Reader Service. From time to time we make our lists of customers available to reputable firms who may have a product or service of interest to you. If you would prefer we not share your name and address, please check here: ☐

LISUS07

Love Inspired®
SUSPENSE

TITLES AVAILABLE NEXT MONTH

Don't miss these four stories in December

HER CHRISTMAS PROTECTOR by Terri Reed

Running from her abusive ex-husband, Faith Delange found shelter in Sisters, Oregon. But how secure was her haven? The longer she stayed, the more she endangered her new friends, including protective rancher Luke Campbell.

BURIED SINS by Marta Perry
The Three Sisters Inn

Caroline Hampton feared her husband was involved in something shady, but he died before she could confront him...didn't he? A string of dangerous incidents implied otherwise. Caroline fled to her sisters' inn, but trouble—and the suspicions of Police Chief Zachary Burkhalter—followed her home....

HARD EVIDENCE by Roxanne Rustand
Snow Canyon Ranch

Human remains were found behind the isolated cabins Janna McAllister was fixing up on her family ranch. And she suspected someone lurked out there even still. Her unexpected lodger, Deputy Sheriff Michael Robertson, made the single mother feel safe. Until she unwittingly tempted a killer out of the woodwork.

BLUEGRASS PERIL by Virginia Smith

When her boss was murdered, the police suspected single mom Becky Dennison. To clear her name, Becky teamed up with Scott Lewis, from a neighboring breeder's farm, to find the truth. In this Kentucky race, the stakes were life or death.

LISCNMI107